Sweet FATE

LAURELIN PAIGE

Hot Alphas. Smart Women. Sexy Stories.

Editing: Erica Russikoff

Proofing: Michele Ficht

Cover: Laurelin Paige

Formatting: Alyssa Garcia

ISBN: 978-1-942835-52-3

Sweet FATE

CHAPTER
One

Dylan

I NOTICED HER the minute she came outside.

She hadn't been in the house when Aaron and I had arrived, almost half an hour earlier. We'd been greeted by Susan and Raymond Kincaid, Donovan's parents, who had cordially shown us to the grounds behind the house where the rest of the guests were waiting. I'd scanned the crowd for her. There were many faces I recognized—mostly employees from Reach, the company I co-owned, but a few were people from the long-ago past when Donovan had been engaged to my stepdaughter. So many familiar acquaintances, but not her.

And she was the only one I cared to see.

I'd spent the next thirty minutes milling about, nursing a too-sweet glass of champagne while pretending to be interested in the small talk of associates and friends. Petty subjects received great attention—the weather, the stock exchange, the latest hit Broadway show, what designer the bride would wear.

I'd perked up when I'd heard that last one. Though I cared not a fig about couture, any mention of Sabrina was of interest. It would be in conjunction with her name that someone might address the whereabouts of her sister, the bride's only family. She had to be here, hadn't she? Would there be anything at all that would keep her away?

Perhaps it wouldn't seem too obvious if I asked Weston. We'd all shared dinner the last time I'd been in the States, rode home in the same car. Surely it would be natural to inquire about that lovely girl...*what was her name?*

I'd considered the best way to broach the subject while Weston's old assistant poked at him.

"Don't talk to me, don't even look at me without that little boy in your arms," Roxie scolded her former boss in her husky Hungarian accent. "I barely got time to be in his life before you take him away."

Weston had responded with a laugh. "He's here, he's here. Calm down. Elizabeth is showing him off to—"

I never did get to hear where Weston's wife had absconded with Weston's son because that's when the woman I'd been waiting for arrived—all rosy-cheeked and glossed lips, her hair knotted loosely at the back of her neck, her eyes twinkling with excitement—and all sound rushed past me like white noise. My vision tunneled to only see her. Audrey Lind. The most beautiful woman in existence.

She was bustling out of the house, the skirt of her dress gathered in one hand so as not to trip. The red wine of her outfit matched the color on her lips and fit her like she'd been sewn into it. Her curves were accentuated with a twisted tie around the waistline and sheer material at her neckline. She must have been locked away inside getting ready all this time. She was a lone ruby in an array of plain stones. It was impossible to miss her presence.

I pinned my eyes to her, watching as she pushed past guests, making her way to the band. She whispered something to the guitar player, who then gave a signal to the singer. The current song was wrapped up, and Audrey stepped up to the microphone.

"Hello, everyone, if I could have your attention…" She waited for the rest of the crowd to catch up to me.

"That's Sabrina's sister, Aubrey," Weston informed Roxie.

"Audrey," I corrected without moving my gaze from the woman in question.

"Right. Audrey. Wasn't that what I said?" It most certainly wasn't what he'd said, but I refrained from arguing. "Real sweet girl."

Sweet, yes. Girl? She was a woman in so many ways that mattered.

And a girl too, I supposed, in ways that mattered more.

With the guests, for the most part, quieted, Audrey continued with her address. "I've just gotten word from the driver that Donovan and Sabrina are about ten minutes away—seven minutes-ish now—and I wanted to tell you all what to expect from here."

"Is there a plan in place for if she says no?" a male voice shouted from the audience.

I knew that voice—Nate Sinclair, another of the men who owned the advertising company with me, Donovan, and Weston. I cringed internally on Audrey's behalf. My eyes left her briefly to find him in the crowd.

A tall brunette clapped her hand over Nate's mouth. His girlfriend, Trish, I assumed. I had yet to meet her. "Don't listen to him!" she cried apologetically. "He thinks he's funny."

"Yes, ignore him, please!" Audrey exclaimed in horror, as I knew she would. "There is no way Sabrina won't say yes, but that's just bad luck to even think such a thing!"

Nate backed down. "Sorry, sorry. Tasteless joke."

"It *is* unusual," Roxie remarked critically at my side. "You think a surprise wedding is okay for the guests, but for the bride?"

I couldn't agree more. Weddings, on the whole, were much ado about nothing. The biggest marketing ploy since the invention of Valentine's Day, if anyone asked me. And I would know. Advertising was my job.

Today, though, I was less impatient with the jollification. Enduring the hoopla was scarcely a hardship when Audrey was the reward.

"As soon as they arrive," she said, picking up where she'd left off. "Sabrina will be whisked to a private room to get ready, and guys, I'm telling you, she is seriously low maintenance. She'll be prettied up in thirty minutes, forty minutes tops. We'll have another announcement to gather everyone in their seats when it's showtime. Until then, feel free to munch on hors d'oeuvre, drink champagne, and dance! Isn't this day amazing?"

A burst of applause followed her speech. Conversations resumed and the band started up once again. Audrey casually made her way back to the house, stopping to greet people on the way. Nearby, a waiter opened a champagne bottle, popping off the cork with a loud crack. She jumped then fell into a fit of laughter as she clutched her hand to her heart.

God, she was enchanting. I couldn't look away. She could light up an already brilliant day. She was incandescent. She absolutely glowed.

"... Dylan, for a toast."

"Hm?" I'd missed the beginning of whatever it was that Weston had said, only tuning in at the sound of my name.

He clapped a hand on my back. "I was just saying we should go up and have a drink with Donovan when they get here."

The only place I wanted to be was alone with Audrey.

But I wasn't counting on having the opportunity, and I'd lost sight of her now, so I turned my full attention to my friend. "Sure. Let me find Aaron so I can tell him where I am."

My son was exactly where I'd left him, curled up with his earbuds and his mobile in the shade on the side of the house. He was a shy thirteen—er, fourteen-year-old; he'd recently had a birthday. I hadn't expected him to want to mingle. He'd only accompanied me, in fact, so that we could continue on to Hartford afterward to stay for a few days. I planned to take him to the Mark Twain House & Museum and the Harriet Beecher Stowe Center. Whether he appreciated it or not, I meant to culture the boy.

Of course I'd also had to agree I'd take him to a video game competition being held over the weekend, but I felt comfortable with the compromise.

I stooped down in front of Aaron. At the sight of me, he pulled a bud from one of his ears. "Is the wedding starting?"

"No, you have another half hour or so."

He gave a fist-bumping motion and picked up the bud as if to return it to his ear, apparently done with the conversation, but I halted him.

"I might be MIA for a bit. I'm going to see if Donovan needs help getting ready. I'll come and get you when it's time."

"Yeah, yeah," he said impatiently, his eyes already back on the screen of his phone.

Well, then. No need to worry about him.

I stood up again, just as another round of applause came from the crowd behind the house. Imagining that signalled Donovan and Sabrina's arrival, I headed inside through the side door to meet up with Weston instead of returning to the backyard.

The Kincaid's country home was large enough to be called an estate. I'd been there before, but not enough times and not recently enough to know my way around the place, especially coming in from an entrance I didn't normally use. I ambled through the halls, my ears perked, listening for sounds to direct me to the lounge.

I was also conscientious of Audrey. If Sabrina was in the house now, her sister surely was as well. When I'd reached the front hall, I froze. Was that her giggle coming faintly from above? I looked up the stairs, hoping to catch her.

"There you are," Nate said, making me jump. He grinned. "Sorry for startling you. I tracked down Donovan. Weston just stepped out to his car to get—"

Just then the front door opened and Weston walked in, carrying a box of Macallan.

"—the Scotch," Nate finished. "And here we all are."

"Shall we?" I asked, still half listening for the beautiful melody of Audrey's laugh.

Nate nodded. "I'll lead the way."

A few minutes later, after swiping four tumblers and a corkscrew from Raymond Kincaid's bar, we were gathered in a downstairs guest room with the groom. Donovan was already mostly dressed in black tuxedo bottoms and a crisp white dress shirt when we'd arrived. Now he was leaning against the windowsill, seemingly relaxed except for the constant twirl of his pocket watch.

A drink would do him well.

Weston handed him a tumbler and broke open the Scotch, then poured two fingers into his glass before turning to fill mine and Nate's.

"A toast!" Weston exclaimed, raising his own drink when he'd finished serving the rest of us. "To Donovan—may all your days be filled with rich love."

"Hear, hear," Nate agreed, and everyone took a sip.

"Look at you—a proper best man," I said to Weston. He was the only groomsman at all, actually, Donovan having figured it was too much of an ordeal to have more with the casual nature of the ceremony.

It was a reasonable decision, and an expected choice, though Weston wasn't generally considered the most responsible of our bunch, and my tone hinted at the fact.

"Shut up. You didn't even bother to come to my wedding," he scoffed.

I shrugged, unwilling to feel any remorse for not attending. "It wasn't a real wedding at the time."

"It was always a real wedding," he insisted. "It wasn't a real marriage."

"Both sound terrible." This remark earned a short laugh from Nate.

Weston wasn't amused. "You're such a grouch. Is this really fair to Donovan on his big day?"

"Donovan knows who I am, and he still thought to invite me." I looked to the man in question and felt validated when he nodded in agreement. "Nate isn't big on these affairs either. Why aren't you poking at him?"

"Because *he* came to my wedding." Weston would never let that go, I was beginning to realize.

"Came *at* your wedding too, from what I heard," Donovan said pointedly.

And now Weston's attention was somewhere besides me. "Nate? Something you'd like to share?"

"Only that I *heard the same* about Donovan." The two exchanged a look, some recognition of an inside joke that was apparently filthy in nature. "But I will say, to your point, Dylan—though it's true I could take or leave the whole marriage tradition, it doesn't mean I'm down on love all together."

The comment was directed toward me, the last single man in the room.

"You're really smitten with this girl you're dating, aren't you?" It wasn't the comment I wanted to make, but I was being polite. For now.

"Trish?" Nate thought a moment. "I love her. I'm in love with her. I basically live with her. We're as married as we're ever going to get, but that doesn't mean we aren't solid."

"Christ, you too? You're daft as a brush, the whole lot of you." Apparently, my civility had expired.

"You must be looking in the mirror, Locke."

"Original, King."

Weston ignored my retort. "You know who's really the dickhole—Cade. He should be here. It's bad enough that he's gone on leave of absence for an eternity. It's another to miss one of your only friend's weddings."

It wasn't the first time today I'd heard him griping about the fifth owner of Reach. "Why are you so cross with him? He came to *your* wedding."

"Eh, not really." He looked to Donovan, as though seeking permission.

Curious, I turned my attention to the groom as well.

Donovan grabbed his vest from the bed where it was draped and turned toward the mirror. "He was in town for other reasons. Attending Weston's wedding was incidental."

There was no doubt that Donovan was watching what he said. I didn't mind people having their own secrets for the most part, but Cade's disappearance from the business had been abrupt. He'd been gone now for almost seven months. It was beginning to be an elephant that no one wanted to address.

"What did he have to do in New York?" It wasn't the day to pry, but I could certainly tiptoe around the subject. Cade rarely ever came to the States. He'd been managing the Tokyo office since Donovan had returned to New York, which meant, at present, there was only an acting manager running the place.

Donovan shrugged as he buttoned his vest.

"You don't know or you're not at liberty to discuss?" I pressed.

"Something like that."

"Uh-huh. Then I'm guessing the reason for his extended leave is also something you aren't at liberty to discuss."

He shifted his eyes toward mine in the reflection and smiled slyly. "Something like that."

Obviously this was going nowhere.

Giving up, I turned to look out the window into the backyard. The guests who had, for the most part, been standing and chatting earlier were now starting to take their seats. I scanned the sea of faces, searching for the one I most wanted to see.

I hadn't yet found her when Weston came to peer over my shoulder. "Looks like people are starting to gather. I'm going to go down now so I can make sure Elizabeth is good with Sebastian before it's time to line up."

Nate finished off his glass. "I'll go with you. Trish gets antsy at these things. I shouldn't leave her alone for too long."

I listened halfheartedly to Weston and Nate bestow congratulations and well-wishes as I continued to study the crowd, looking always for her. She'd said it was kismet when we'd met before. I didn't believe in that nonsense, not anymore.

But if she were outside right now...if she looked up and our eyes met...

"She's helping Sabrina get ready," Donovan said.

I looked back and was startled to find we were now the only two in the room. Meaning Donovan had been addressing me. But he couldn't have guessed who I'd been looking for. Could he?

"Who?" I asked innocently.

"Audrey."

As I'd assumed, and yet, still I'd searched.

"That is why you're here, isn't it? I can't imagine any other reason you'd attend a wedding, let alone fly across an ocean for one. Had to be to see her."

I threw him a scowl. "Poppycock. I was coming to the States anyway to see Aaron." And yes, also to see Audrey. Not to start anything or have some glorious reunion, but after seven months of pining, I'd hoped seeing her might knock the want of her out of my system.

I wasn't about to tell any of that to Donovan though.

Too late, I realized my defensiveness had caused me to respond incorrectly. "But if I hadn't already planned to be here to see Aaron, I'd have come anyway. For you. I'd never miss *your* nuptials."

"Uh-huh." He smirked like he was in on a joke. "She's graduated now, you know. Looking for work."

"Who?" I could play this game all day.

He threw me a glare that reminded me he could play all day too, then went about tucking his tie into his vest. "There are ways to influence where she ends up. I'd be happy to help if…"

"'Influence where she ends up?' Whatever is that supposed to mean?"

"That if you want her close to you, it's possible to make that happen."

I wanted to ask more about those possibilities, wanted to pursue them sincerely. While I couldn't know what Donovan had in mind, I did trust that he could do what he said. He was a man who made things happen, and wasn't it tempting to pounce on his offer? To live a life where I saw Audrey Lind every day? I couldn't imagine anything more miraculous.

But I was a pragmatic man. Even if a woman like her would want a man nearly twenty years older than she was, we were on different paths. Especially now that she'd finished school. She had her entire future ahead of her. Who was I, with those days long in my past, to step in and hold her back?

"I'm not moving back to New York," I said, my jaw set. "And if you're offering something else, I'm definitely not interested in that."

"Are you sure about that?"

Yes. As miserable as that made me, I was sure.

But why was Donovan pushing us together anyway? I'd assumed he didn't know anything about me and Audrey.

Did he?

I turned my full attention on him and narrowed my eyes. "What exactly are you suggesting is between she and I, might I ask?"

"I'm suggesting nothing."

"It sure sounds like you're suggesting something," I grumbled.

He picked up his tuxedo jacket from the bed and paused. "Such as?"

"Such as some imagined relationship between me and your soon-to-be sister-in-law."

"Nope. Not suggesting anything of the sort." He slid one arm through the sleeve of the jacket, followed by the other.

"I'd appreciate it if you continued that way." What on earth had provoked this conversation in the first place? Had I given any indication that I was interested in the girl or had he simply been fishing?

More importantly, had I confirmed anything if he had been? I quickly replayed everything that had been said in my head. A frown sunk on my lips. "No one needs to know about this conversation, either. Including Sabrina."

Donovan stood in front of the mirror again, fidgeting with his collar, but stopped to consider me. "Are you asking me to keep something from my wife?"

That had been what I'd implied, hadn't it? Perhaps that wasn't fair. Especially since my own marriage had been destroyed with secrets and lies.

A thought suddenly occurred to me. "Has Audrey ever...has she mentioned...me? To you or Sabrina?"

"A shared kiss. Nothing else."

That shouldn't have been as disappointing as it was. I hadn't told anyone about Audrey, after all. Not even about the kiss.

But I was a different beast than she. I wasn't prone to gushing and prattling on about such things, whereas she was. If there was anything to gush and prattle on about, it was hard to believe she'd be able to bottle it in.

"Good," I said, trying for nonchalant. "Because there's nothing besides that for her to mention. Which is why there's nothing to mention to Sabrina either. It's not asking you to keep something from your wife if she already knows all there is to begin with."

He turned to face me, again with that knowing smirk. "Sure. Whatever you say."

Worried that wasn't the end of it, I changed the subject myself. "Enough about me. This is your day." I stood back to size him up. "You look good! Are you nervous?"

"Not since the Scotch kicked in."

"Sounds about right." Though it didn't need it, I reached out to straighten his tie. It was an excuse for an intimate moment. "You took a long time to get here. You deserve this, my friend."

"Misery and woe?"

I really had been a shithead, spreading my doom and gloom all over his big event.

With a sigh, I attempted to steer a new course. "That's how it worked out for me, but perhaps I'm not a man who knows how to hold onto happiness."

"Never too late to learn."

Maybe that was true. Maybe I could find joy with a woman once again. Maybe this time I could keep it in my grasp, protect it, never let it go.

I didn't believe that rubbish, however. I didn't subscribe to the fancies of fairy tales or the notion that happily ever after could exist.

But despite my skepticism, I said, "Then show me how it's done, will you?" Because on Donovan's wedding day, I was a good enough friend to pretend it was possible.

CHAPTER
Two

IT WAS A BEAUTIFUL wedding, considering that it was, in fact, a wedding.

Sabrina had chosen a tailored gown with sleek lines and a plunging neckline. An oversized bow trailed to the floor behind her, adding just a hint of drama. Her eyes glistened throughout the ceremony, and her face wore a smile that reached from ear to ear.

It was difficult not to remember that Amanda had once been slated to stand where she was, and it added a bittersweet flavor to an event that already tasted tart in my mouth.

Donovan remained stoic as always, but he gave his own hints at emotion. The shallow rise and fall of his chest, the tightening of his throat while reciting his vows. His gaze never left hers, as though he were chained to her through their eyes. It was obvious he loved her, that he worshipped the ground she walked on, and I imagined for those reasons that he considered this the best day of his life.

I hoped, for both their sakes, more best days would

follow.

I watched them intently, paying attention to every exchange between them, to every soft word whispered, every slight touch. Focusing completely on them was the only way to keep from sneaking glances at the bride's sister. The only look at her I'd allowed myself had been when she'd walked down the aisle ahead of Sabrina, when *everyone*'s eyes were on her.

But even without giving her my direct focus, I saw her. She stood to the side of Sabrina the entire wedding. She was there in my periphery, her presence pulling at me like she was an industrial strength magnet and I, an iron rod. She kept herself together, neither fidgeting nor breaking down in happy tears, but I could sense the joy inside her, wanting to burst. I could feel it as if it were an emotion coming from inside myself. I could feel her as though she were in my arms and not five meters away.

After the kiss between the bride and groom and the proclamation of man and wife, Donovan and Sabrina were pulled aside by the photographer while Audrey resumed the spot behind the microphone. She directed everyone to the tent where dinner was soon to be served, informing guests how to find their assigned seats. Then she was swept away with the fluster of activity, and I lost sight of her again.

For the best.

I didn't want to know who she was with, who might have come as her date. I didn't want to hear the laughs she shared with others and not with me. I didn't want to see her *not* looking for me. So instead I looked for Aaron.

I managed for a good part of the evening to stay occupied with my son. Through dinner and the cutting of the cake and most of the toasts. Then it was her turn to raise her champagne glass and deliver her blessings, and then I had to look again.

"For those who don't know, Sabrina is as much a mother to me as she is a sister," she said. "Our dad died when I was thirteen, and mom had been gone a while by then. And this woman—this wonderful, beautiful woman—changed her entire life to look out for me."

She choked up and had to pause, dabbing at her eyes, until she could talk again. "I've been so very lucky to have her devotion. So lucky to be loved by her. She deserves every bit of happiness and affection that she spent on me to be returned to her with interest, and I know Donovan is the man who can deliver. I wish you everything your heart desires, sis. You deserve it. And no more worrying about me. You've been the best example, and I only hope that if or when I find a love as amazing as you've found with Donovan, that I have the ability to recognize it."

She mouthed some form of I love you and blew a kiss, and I closed my eyes and tried to figure out why her gorgeous speech left a pit in my stomach. Certainly I worried that Donovan and Sabrina wouldn't last, that years later they'd look back on today as a bitter memory and despise every shallow sentiment that had been spoken.

But concern wasn't the feeling twisting in my gut. This burned more like jealousy. Yes, yes, I was jealous—of Donovan and Sabrina who were at the beginning of their happy days, for their love, still pure and untainted. Jealous of Audrey and her ability to be so genuinely candid. But most of all, jealous of whomever it was that she was waiting to find, the man who would get to love her and feel her love in return.

I took a deep breath in and let it out. This was ridiculous. *I* was ridiculous. If I wanted the girl so badly, why didn't I just go talk to her? What was keeping me from her?

Only myself, that was who.

After the toasts had finished, I left Aaron in a passionate discussion with Weston about some animated show called Voltron and went to find her. I discovered her at the punch bowl, patiently listening while Donovan's mother rattled on about the disappointments of the day. That wasn't a conversation I wanted to be in the middle of, so I stood nearby, waiting for them to wrap up.

I saw when she noticed me.

Her forehead, which had just a moment before been creased, relaxed and her brows rose. Did I imagine that her eyes sparked? That her entire face lit up?

"Dylan!" she exclaimed when she was finally free of Susan Kincaid.

Without reservation, she moved in to wrap me in her embrace, and my entire being sighed with relief. She smelled just as I'd remembered—like apples and bourbon, like spring and vibrancy. Her touch sent warmth shooting through my limbs. And the feel of her, the weight of her in my arms, was like finding gravity. Like discovering the best ballast. Like being firmly anchored after too long adrift at sea.

It was a brief harbor.

Too soon she was stepping back, putting an acceptable distance between us.

"I saw you earlier," she said, and I clung to every syllable she uttered. "I confess—I'd been looking, and I meant to come over, but then I'd get distracted or you'd be with your son, and I worried about intruding."

Then she had looked for me. I could feel the span of my chest increasing with that knowledge.

"It never seemed like the proper time," I agreed.

"I'm glad you're here now. It's so good to see you."

"You as well." Silence stretched between us, a comfortable quiet that kept our gazes locked while all the words I couldn't say effervesced inside me like champagne bubbles pressing at the cork. She smiled as though she understood what I hadn't spoken. Her cheeks pinked, and finally she broke our gaze with a quick glance at her feet.

"How are you?" she said when she looked back up.

At the same time, I asked, "You've been well?"

She laughed, that angelic tinkle that always made me heady.

"Go on," I offered. I would have said nothing at all for the rest of our interaction, content to simply listen to every one of her precious sounds.

She swept a stray piece of hair behind her ear. "Things are good with you? And Aaron?"

"Yes, we're good. He's grown more than three inches since Thanksgiving, at least two since I saw him in the spring. He curses more than a child should probably curse in front of his father, and he is glued to his phone…" *Shut it, will you? She doesn't want to hear about your parenting woes.* "But we're both good."

"Except you're at a wedding—are you completely miserable?"

"Not completely." Far from at this particular moment. "And you? You're finished with your master's, I presume. How goes the art conversation?"

She smiled at my purposeful switch of the word *con-*

versation for *conservation.* "I am done. Walked the stage three weeks ago. Now I'm doing the find-a-job thing, which is almost as dreadful as school was. I started applying months ago, and well, you know art conservation is a real specialized career. Entry-level work isn't spectacular. I'm still building a portfolio and all." She twisted her bottom lip between her teeth. "But! I do have a second interview at the Boston Museum of Fine Arts. Jax and I are driving out there tomorrow." She glanced toward a young man sitting at a table, drawing with a stylus onto a digital pad.

I didn't want to ask. I didn't want to know.

"Boston Museum of Fine Arts? That's fantastic!"

She blushed again. "It's only an interview."

"It's still fantastic." I couldn't help myself—I asked. "And Jax is…?"

She nodded toward the man. "We went to school together. Jax is a digital artist. We're thinking of maybe getting a place together if I end up somewhere 'cool.' His words."

The burn of jealousy returned, acidic in my stomach. "He's a boyfriend, then?"

"No, no," she said quickly. "A friend."

As if sensing he was being talked about, Jax looked up from his iPad and gave Audrey a smile. It was the same kind of smile that I imagined I gave her—adoring and full of want.

"He likes you more than a friend," I said, my throat scalding with the words.

"Ah, no. Well…" Her eyes darted down again. "Maybe. We'll see."

The floor felt like it was plummeting beneath my feet. Of course she'd have a beau. Who could know her and let her get away?

"But I am excited about the possibility," she said eagerly, apparently unaware that I was sinking into despair. "Boston isn't that far away from New York, and especially if Sabrina starts having babies, I'm going to want to be close. I need to live vicariously through her until I get some of my own."

"You want children?" This shouldn't have been a surprise.

"Definitely. I'm one of those greedy women who want it all—a fulfilling career, an adoring husband, *and* a brood. I'm thinking five is a good number. But maybe I'll squeeze out six."

"Six?"

"Like I said, a brood."

A brood. She wanted a brood.

I spent my days dreaming of retirement and putting my teenager through college. At my age, perhaps, one baby could be considered. Two, if I worked fast. Certainly not five. Not six. Not *a brood*.

This was what was keeping me from her—this vast chasm that stood between her future trajectory and mine. She was at the start of her life, when girls wanted marriage and family and white picket fences. And why shouldn't she want those things? She had many years ahead of her to want it all. Many years to *have* it all.

I would be nothing but an obstacle for her dreams.

If she were even to want me.

So though I yearned to ask her to dance, to press my

face into the curve of her neck and hold her tight against me, I didn't extend the offer.

"Of course, I have to find the right guy first," she said, twisting her hands in front of her. "Who knows? Maybe I already know him."

"Maybe it's Jax."

"Yeah. Maybe."

She opened her mouth to say something else when Sabrina's voice cut through the noise of the crowd. "All right, ladies. I'm throwing the bouquet!"

Audrey clasped her hands at her heart. "The bouquet! That's my cue." She stepped forward and placed a soft kiss on my cheek, a kiss that I was sure I'd feel for the rest of my life. "This wasn't so terribly awkward, after all," she said when she pulled away.

"No, not terribly awkward, after all."

My eyes didn't leave her as she walked away. Inside, a vice gripped my ribs, squeezing all the air from my lungs, splitting my chest in two, and still I watched her with a smile pasted on my lips.

It wasn't entirely fake. It *did* make me happy to see her, even while seeing her taught me the most wretched lesson—though I could never have her, though we were fated to be two ships that passed in the night, Audrey Lind was not a woman I was getting over anytime soon.

CHAPTER
Three

"THANK FUCK IT'S finally stopped raining. I'd forgotten what the sun looked like." Amy threw back the last of her Diet Coke and stepped away from the window to toss the can in my recycling bin. Then she perched on the corner of my desk, a habit she was wont to do when she intruded on my lunch hour as she was doing now.

Honestly, I didn't mind all that much. Though I was the head of the London office, I mainly took care of the finances, a rather isolated job. Amelia Rahim—Amy—managed our sales division. She was bullheaded, cold-hearted, and churlish. We got along splendidly.

"I didn't take you as one who complained about dreary weather. Isn't grey your favorite color? You sure wear it often enough." I grabbed the stack of month-end reports that were stacked precariously near her bottom and moved them to a safer location on my desk before returning my focus to my screen.

"Grey, charcoal, nickel, jet—all shades of black, really. I like my outside to match my in." She picked up the Granny Smith sitting next to my computer and bounced it up and down in the palm of her hand. "And I do love it when the sky takes on my moods, but I'd prefer to do without the wet. My hair frizzes." She caught the apple, brought it to her mouth, and took a crisp bite.

"I was planning on eating that," I grumbled.

"You were taking too long to get to it."

"I suppose you need to eat healthy more than I do, at your age." Amy was the one employee on the management team older than me. Though it was only by three days, I didn't often let her forget it.

"You're a real barrel of laughs today, Locke. Considering you've been moody as all get out for the past several months, I have to ask what's up. Has the sun gotten to you too?"

I looked up from my work to gaze out the window at the clear sky. Frankly, I hadn't noticed the weather was any different today from any other day. Since I'd returned from the States this summer, it had seemed that it didn't matter if the sun was shining or not. Every day of the past three and a half months had been dreary and bland.

I was well aware of the problem. It was Audrey. She'd ruined me when I'd seen her again. I'd been reminded that she was the brightest light in existence. Everything else was dull in comparison.

Amy's remark was the first indication that anyone else had picked up on my sullenness, though. I'd been too self-absorbed to think about my mood's effect on others.

And *was* I feeling less solemn today?

I did a quick body scan, and yes, indeed, my chest felt less tight. The corners of my mouth were relaxed instead of turned down. My shoulders didn't feel weighed down with an unbearable heaviness.

Why I was feeling better, I had no idea. Maybe the sun actually had made a difference.

I turned my attention back to my computer. "It's our numbers," I said, an answer that sounded as good as any other. "As of right now, this quarter is up twenty-two percent from last."

"We are? Damn. I had no idea. And here you were so certain that the new French location would put a dent in business."

"It was a reasonable assumption," I said defensively. We'd had three rather large international clients that had taken their business to Weston's Paris office since it was more central to their headquarters. But after I'd complained about it thoroughly a number of times, Amy had decided to do something about it and found us a number of good-paying clients to take their place. "It's all your doing, really. You deserve the congratulations."

"Not just my doing. If you hadn't moaned so loudly about the situation, I would have continued the method that has worked well for me so far in life—doing as little as possible."

I looked up to see if she was serious before breaking into laughter. Amy was a workaholic like no other. She ate, slept, and breathed Reach, Inc. She had practically no social life or hobbies, unless crushing the competition counted. She often claimed she'd never married because she believed in monogamy, and she was already married to her job.

"See what I mean? A couple of days ago, I don't think you would have caught the joke."

"What a shame that would have been." I finished entering the numbers on the report. The totals wouldn't be accurate until we got confirmation that the deposits had gone through, but I liked to have an estimate as soon as the quarter was finished. "There we are. Twenty-two point three percent growth, to be more specific."

"We're a good team, Dylan. We should celebrate. It's been awhile since we've done that—just you and I." Her meaning was clear, but she crossed one leg over the other to enunciate her point.

I couldn't help watching. The woman had long limbs that she kept well-toned. I'd had them wrapped around me on more than one occasion. Apparently, she was offering to wrap them around me again.

While I didn't generally like the idea of sex with co-workers, Amy's commitment to no-commitment was as steadfast as mine. We were the perfect pair, only in it for the benefits. Often, it was easier to turn to her than go to a pub and try to hit on a stranger.

It *had* been awhile since I'd last hooked up with anyone. Not since before Audrey. I hadn't been interested, and it hadn't crossed my mind to think that maybe sleeping with another woman would be helpful. Perhaps it would help get me over my fixation on the girl.

And yet...

I paused too long with a response. "Think about it," Amy said, jumping down from my desk. "I'm here all afternoon. You can tell me if you're interested at the end of the day."

"I'll do that." Was I stupid for not jumping on her offer right away? We'd always had an uncomplicated arrangement in the past. Finish up in the office, leave together, and then... "Oh, Amy!" I called before she'd made it out of my office. "I just remembered. I'm meeting with that Lieber guy this afternoon. So you may be here all afternoon, but I won't."

"The car manufacturer? You've already met with him twice. He's not coming to the office?" Amy's tone said she was as annoyed with Hans Lieber as I was. The man brought prospects of a huge addition to the firm's accounts—which was fantastic. But his insistence on continuing to meet with an owner of Reach was beyond irritating. I was not the person who closed the sales. That was Amy's job.

That didn't mean I couldn't do it. It meant I didn't want to.

But I would. "He only has a limited time in his schedule to meet so he asked if I could come to his hotel. He's staying at the Corinthia."

Amy cringed. "How pompous."

"Yes. Very."

"But also, seems the man has money he wants to spend. Want me to come with? I could rearrange my afternoon."

I considered. "No, not this time. I think he's right on the verge of signing on, and I don't want to give him any reason to change his mind."

"Because meeting me might just be the best reason to run," she said. I rushed to amend what I'd said, but she put up a hand to halt me. "No worries. I'm joking. I get it. Take the meeting, and then text me and let me know if you'd like that celebratory dinner. My house. I'll even order takeout."

I laughed and agreed to text her later. I'd even think more about actually saying yes to her offer. After all, it would probably be good for me to have a little fun, reason to celebrate or not.

Four hours later, I walked out of the Corinthia Hotel with another reason to celebrate—Hans Lieber had only wanted to meet to tell me he officially wanted to hire Reach for his international campaigns. The contracts had to be written up and there would be more negotiating of fine details, but the deal felt solid. Irritating as the man might be, he had a reputation of integrity, and a handshake was as reliable as any signed paper.

It was definitely a win that made me feel good. There was practically a spring in my step as I walked toward Whitehall to hail a cab. At the corner, something came over me—a strange sense of whimsy that made me change my mind about the car. The weather was so nice, the temperature unusually warm for the first of October, that I decided to walk through the park instead. Then I could jump on the underground at St. James's Park Station.

The detour was the perfect choice. The trees were beautifully clothed in autumn colors. Red, yellow, and orange leaves dressed the walkways as well. I listened for them to crunch under my feet, but they were still too rain-soaked from the previous week's weather. Instead the air was filled with the sound of birds and kids. Most of the deck chairs were occupied. The sunshine had obviously called more than just me to the outdoors. And why wouldn't it? St. James's Park was magnificent. I'd forgotten how much so. How long had it been since I'd strolled through its gardens? How long since I'd strolled through any gardens at all?

I couldn't remember.

I lingered on my way, breathing the fresh air, and wished there was someone to share the experience with.

No, that was a lie. I didn't wish for someone—I wished for Audrey, as I'd wished for her so often over the last several months, and even before the wedding, since the week we spent together in New York. Nothing had changed in my philosophies because of her. I still believed love was miserable and ended in arguments with overpriced solicitors. I still held that I'd rather live alone than mess with that bullshit again.

But I also yearned for her. I wished for her companionship. I wanted her to talk to, to hold at night. I dreamed her everywhere around me. I thought I saw her every time there was a crowd—on the underground, at the market. Over there, watching the mallards at the edge of the lake.

I stopped short and stared.

My imagination was getting the best of me because the profile of that woman really did look like Audrey. From the high cheekbones to the point of her chin to the amber color of her hair. Even the boots she wore looked identical to the ones Audrey had worn in New York. I needed to get closer to really tell. I took a step toward her. Then another tentative step.

Suddenly, the woman turned in my direction, and I quickly looked away, not wanting to be caught staring. I hadn't just been staring, either—I'd been creeping up on her. What the bloody hell was that about? My obsession was going too far, stalking strangers in the park. Audrey was not in Westminster. She was somewhere far away. Boston, maybe. Definitely not here.

I resumed my walk, leaving behind the stupid fantasies

of my deluded mind.

But then a familiar voice called after me. "Dylan? Dylan *Locke*? Is that you?"

I turned slowly, cautiously.

And there she was—*my* angel, my light, my Audrey.

"It *is* you!" she exclaimed with a clap before bounding toward me. She wrapped me up in a ferocious hug. "I can't believe it! I mean, I *can* because that's the way it is between us. But I didn't know when it would happen, and I'm so happy that it's happened today, of all days!"

My heart was pounding like a bass drum, and though I hated it when she let go of me, I was relieved she wouldn't hear it trying to escape from my chest. I had so many questions, and I meant to ask every single one of them as soon as the air returned to my lungs.

"Audrey—what are you doing here? Are you on vacation?" I tried to ignore what it meant that she hadn't contacted me about her visit.

"No, I live here! Isn't it crazy? I thought about calling you, but I was an idiot and lost my phone right when I got here and when I got the new one, a bunch of the contacts didn't transfer over, including yours, and then I thought maybe that was best because I didn't want to be weird, reaching out uninvited, and I figured if we were meant to see each other we would, and look! We did!" She was excited, her words bubbling out of her so rapidly I had a hard time keeping up.

In fact, I was still stuck on the first part of her monologue. "Did you say you *live* here?"

"I did! I got a job! Today was my first day, which was an experience that I can't even begin to describe, and then it's the first day it's been sunny since I moved here, so I came to the park on a whim, and here you are! It's kismet!"

I felt lightheaded.

And happy. Really fucking happy.

"Yes, kismet." I almost believed it myself.

"Then it's settled. We'll have dinner." There she was with that fierce confidence I adored so much. "Are you free tonight?"

I already had my phone out of my pocket so I could shoot a quick text to Amy.

DYLAN: I'm going to have to pass on your offer. Something else has come up.

I hit SEND and looked up to Audrey with a smile. "I'm completely free. Let's do it."

CHAPTER
Four

I DIDN'T BELIEVE this changed things.

Audrey was in town—living here—and I was elated, but I didn't think that I'd suddenly become the right man for her. I didn't instantaneously believe that love was the answer or that I should give a committed relationship another try. I wasn't that naïve.

I simply wanted right then to spend time with her, in whatever way possible. It was selfish and greedy, one of those live-in-the-moment moments. There wasn't thought of repercussions or what happens next or what living near her might mean. Nothing mattered but being in her presence *now*.

"Where shall we go?" she asked, her eyes wide and sparkling as though I might suggest we dine at the palace. "You know the area better than I do."

I really didn't. As most who lived in London, I didn't make it out to the touristy spots all that often.

But I wasn't completely ignorant of the area. "There are a lot of nice restaurants around here because of the museum and Buckingham. The Blue Boar is nice. Or the Roux at Parliament Square." I'd taken clients to both on an occasion or two.

She frowned and looked down at her denim dress and striped tights. "I'm not fit for fancy. Is eating at St. James's Café a cliché?"

I tilted my head, giving serious thought to the question. "I wouldn't say it's cliché to eat at the park café when you're already in the park, but I wouldn't recommend that particular park café. Not anymore. It used to be rather nice. Now it's cafeteria style."

"Ew. No, thanks."

I was out of alternatives. "We could walk and find something?"

She agreed, and we headed toward my initial destination—the park underground stop. I wanted to stare at her as we walked, to catalog every feature and compare it to what I had stored in memory. Somehow I kept my wits about me and focused on the brilliant streaks of pink and orange as the sun set instead, but I listened intently to the melody of her voice as it swirled around me like a crisp autumn leaf caught on the wind.

"I really didn't think this day could get any more beautiful or surreal. It was already mindblowing to get to go into areas of the museum that were for authorized personnel only. I got to look at a Bellini under a microscope. An actual Bellini! I really have to learn to stop putting limits on what the universe has in store for me."

She was like a missionary for the romantics. She proclaimed her gospel every chance she got, and her enthusiasm for her religion was nearly contagious.

I bet she made lots of converts.

I almost wished I could be one of them.

"So you said you worked your first day today? Where are you employed? What happened to Boston?" Not that I wanted her to be in Boston. I didn't want her anywhere else but here.

"Boston turned out to be a bust." She rolled her eyes indicating how dreadful she considered the situation. "They were interested in me, but it was basically an unpaid internship. There was a daily stipend, but it was so small it wouldn't have even covered my coffee requirements. So it worked out when they didn't offer. I was pretty bummed about it at first. I didn't have any real attachments to the city, it's just...Sabrina had left the Boston area to come home and take care of me when Dad died and I had this idea that, if I lived there as an adult, it would somehow bring everything full-circle. It would make her feel like everything was worth it."

That made me frown. "Do you worry she doesn't think her life has been worth it?" I'd only met Sabrina a handful of times now, but she had always struck me as someone quite content with the road she'd taken.

She slowed her stride to think about it. "I guess sometimes I do, but I know she'd never say that. She's only ever said she would have done anything for me, and I believe her. Maybe I wanted it for me. So that I could stop feeling guilty about everything she's sacrificed. But c'est la vie. And like I said, I had no idea there were better opportunities in store."

I glanced over at her and our eyes caught. There was still a very real pull between us. There was no denying it. Her body gravitated toward mine as we walked. Her fingers brushed against mine more than once, each time shocking me with an intensity that sent my heart racing.

The tension trapped in our gaze alone was nearly unbearable.

I couldn't stand it. I looked away.

"The job you have now is a good one, then?" I asked, trying to find more solid ground.

"Well...it *can* be." She stuck her hands into the front pockets of her dress, making her look even younger than she was. "It's another internship, but this time it's paid, and when it's over, if they like me, I'll get to stay. I haven't even told you where the job is—The National Gallery! Can you believe it? I can barely believe it myself and I was there all day! The freaking National Gallery in London. Oh, and the project they have me working on is amazing. It's called Christmas through Art. I'm supposed to catalog and put in chronological order all of the pieces the museum has that might fit into that display. It's quite a task. It will go up the beginning of December, and they'll want me until it goes back down. Beginning of January at least."

The beginning of January, was that all? Not even four months away.

It felt entirely too soon.

I stopped in front of a pub that called itself The Feathers. It seemed as good as any. "Is this okay?"

She looked up at the restaurant as though she'd forgotten we were even looking for one. "It's perfect. I love pub food."

We went inside and got a seat. After a few minutes looking over the menu, I went up to the counter to place our order. I came back with two glasses of red wine.

"Wine. Good idea," she said, raising her glass up in the air. "What shall we toast to?"

"Your new job? Your new living situation?" I'd toast to her, if it were appropriate. To her rich brown eyes that looked like tiger's eye in the right light and her mouth that curved up on one side while she spoke. To her constant smile and the hypnotic sound of her voice. To the way she lived life so fully, so genuinely. The way she let herself be vulnerable and soft yet never diminished her strength.

"How about a toast to us?" she asked as if there could be no other choice. "To finding each other in a city with millions of people."

She clinked her glass to mine, and for just a moment it felt like we really had found each other. Felt like, until she'd called my name in that damn park, I'd been lost.

And hadn't I been?

"To finding each other," I echoed, before bringing the wine to my lips. It was sweeter than I had expected, and heavy, slipping slowly down my throat like honey, leaving traces of itself as it went.

"It's good," Audrey said after taking her own first sip. She took another then set the glass down and laced her fingers together on the table in front of her. "So, Dylan, how did you happen to be st St. James? Do you live nearby? Do you go there a lot? I like the idea of imagining you walking through every day after work, though that's probably more in line with my personality than yours."

Years ago that would have been me as well. Back when I didn't measure time in dollars. When I still thought things would work out in the end.

And today it had been me again.

I scratched the back of my head trying to remember the exact circumstances of how that had come to be. "Actually, it was rather on a whim." I told her about my meeting with Hans Lieber and the weeks of rain and about how I'd decided spur of the moment to take the longer route home.

She slapped the table so hard that her wine sloshed. "I told you it was kismet! That was fate nudging you in the right direction. Did you realize it? I'm so glad you were open enough to hear it!"

"Or, well, it was a rather happy coincidence." It was almost cruel to disagree, but I did have a reputation to attend to.

She glowered at me, but didn't let my refute get her down. "And! And you had no plans! I'm sure your schedule keeps you very busy. How was it that you were available tonight of all nights?"

I didn't tell her that I had a tentative fuck date set with Amy, and that usually my nights were quiet and dull, spent at home logged into the office computer via the cloud. "Yes. That was fortunate indeed."

"Then if you were going to the St. James's Park stop, you must live... No, no!" she halted me when I attempted to tell her. "Let me look at the tube map and see if I can guess." She pulled out her phone and entered the passcode. A couple more swipes and she was puzzling over her screen. "Tower Hill? That's on the same line."

"Wrong direction. Sloane Square would have been my stop. I live between there and South Kensington."

"Ah, of course! Trust Fund Wankers."

"I beg your pardon?"

She laughed, so hard she snorted. "Oh my God, that's humiliating. I'm sorry. It was this internet meme I saw. It had all of London's neighborhoods broken into stereotypes. Most of them, the ones that had anything to do with money especially, had Wankers at the end. Like, this area we're in, I believe, was the Civil Servant Wankers or Political Wankers."

"I see. Quite appropriate."

"And the park is for Tourists and Corgis. Corgis!" She was still laughing.

"You really studied this meme."

"It was a very helpful resource to learning the town. Don't knock it. Where's your office? Let's see if it fits too."

She was too new to know locations by address. I tried to think of the closest landmark she might recognize. "You know where Tottenham Court is? Reach is near there "

"Yes, yes! That's the Media Wankers!"

"It is not."

"It is! Look it up if you don't believe me." Her smile went from ear to ear, and I wanted nothing more than to kiss it off of her and lick the taint of wine from her lips. "Do you want me to pull it up?"

She started to flip through her phone again, but I stopped her. "I believe you. I do. It's just so accurate." I took another sip of the wine before casually asking, "Where do you live? Not too far, I hope. For commute purposes." As though there were any other reason I'd be curious about where she resided, where she spent her evenings and weekends. Where she slept and showered and dreamed.

"Not too far. Lamberth. Between Elephant and Kennington. Basically the Recent Graduates with Poorly Paid Jobs section of town. That's from the meme too."

This time I couldn't help but join in with the laughter. "Oh bloody hell. It's too good."

"Isn't it?"

Our food arrived then, fish and chips for Audrey, meat pies for myself. We dug in, and our conversation transformed into commentary on the tastes and smells of British food.

She also thought everything was called by a ridiculous name. "Soldiers, mashers, Toad in a Hole," she said at one point. "Bubble and Squeak. Welsh Rarebit."

"Don't forget Spotted Dick."

She nearly lost it at that. "I can't handle it. It's so funny!" When she stopped her hooting, she wiped tears from her eyes and said, "All your food sounds like it was named in an attempt to get a stubborn child to eat, I swear."

"I think some of it might have been named to get grown men to eat it, unfortunately."

She shook her head at that, her face still lit in amusement.

God, she was beautiful. As beautiful as my country's food's names were ridiculous.

When our meal was half eaten and a comfortable lull had settled between us, my mind wandered back to something she'd said when we'd been walking, something that had niggled at me ever since.

"You said you'll have a chance to keep on at the Gallery. Is that what you want to do? Stay here in London?" I practically held my breath for her answer.

She took her time giving it, waiting until she'd finished the morsel she was chewing and taking a swig from her drink before saying, "I don't know. I mean, I just got here so I don't have a good sense of whether or not it's home for long. The work itself is incredible, of course. It will look good on my resume if they choose to keep me on or not."

"Wow," I said, unable to come up with another word for what I wanted to say. My breathing resumed, but it was unsteady. I'd never been comfortable with unknowns, and right now, it felt like I was sitting across from a big giant question mark. Would she stay, would she go? Would I miss her as terribly if she left again as I'd missed her before today?

Would I miss her more?

But this wasn't about me. Her being here was all about her.

"I should say congratulations," I realized suddenly. "I'm sorry I didn't say it earlier."

She twirled a chip between her fingers. "Thanks. You know the funny thing—I don't even remember applying for this job specifically. You would think I'd remember a notice from the Gallery. But I applied for so many positions. I'm not sure I even read half of them by the end."

Oh, God. Did I smell a whiff of Donovan Kincaid's hand in her being here? Maybe it wasn't all about her after all. It wasn't beyond him to interfere. He was a man who pulled strings. If he'd intervened when I'd asked him not to, he was truly crossing a line.

I didn't want to jump to conclusions, but I vowed to speak to him about it as soon as possible.

"It all worked out," Audrey said, happily, and I could feel any concern about the how of her being here slipping away. "Because I got one of the best opportunities available. And if things go how I hope..." Her face wrinkled up like she'd had a stray thought and was following it on an absurd journey. "I guess the answer to your question about whether or not I want to stay here has to do with everything else. Like, I don't really have a preference about where I live. Right now my life is about making the best choices possible to keep me on a good career path and about finding The Guy. I'm ready for him. Ready to settle down, get married. Start a family."

I nearly choked on my turkey pie. "Settle down? Already? You're twenty-three!"

She pointed a chip in my direction. "Hey, I'm twenty-four now." As though that made any difference. "And this can't be any sort of a surprise. I have to start early if I'm going to get all those babies in."

Oh, right. All those babies.

Which brought me to a question I'd been avoiding. "What happened to that guy from the wedding?" His name was Jax. I hadn't forgotten. I just refused to use his name if I didn't have to.

"Jax? He was just a friend. Nothing more ever came out of that."

I tried not to be happy about how blaise she sounded about it. But I failed.

"He's dating another friend of ours now. Greg."

"Oh. He's gay." This relieved me even more.

"Pansexual," she corrected.

I had to set my fork down for this. "Jax is transexual?"

She laughed, and I wasn't sure she wasn't making fun of me. "*Pan*sexual. Not trans. It means who he loves isn't limited to a specific gender or gender identity."

"I see. In my day they called that bisexual."

She shook her head at me. "My day still has bisexuals. That's a different thing. That's being attracted to people from two genders. Pansexuals are attracted to people of all genders."

"And here I thought there were only two genders." I was thoroughly confused now and about ready to look around for cameras. This had to be one of those prank shows, didn't it. Someone—Weston probably—had set this whole thing up. Her being here. This conversation about new versions of sexuality.

Again she laughed. "Gender's more complicated than that, it turns out."

And she dropped it. No one jumped out from a hiding spot in the sidelines. She just went back to dipping her fish into her tartar sauce.

So, not a prank. Just me being from a completely different generation. Completely out of her league.

I sighed. "I'll have you know, I feel very old right now."

"Nah. Don't. This is all really new stuff."

"Oh. Good to know." I suddenly wondered if Aaron was as up to date on all this "new stuff." Certainly his mother wasn't.

And what about Audrey? "Are you...do you consider yourself...one of those?"

"Pansexual? I'd like to say I am, in theory. Because I love that notion of being able to love anyone, regardless of what's between their legs. But I'm as straight as they come. A disappointment to my generation, I'm afraid."

It was my turn to laugh. "I'm sure you're not the only heterosexual human your age." I shook my head, and attempted to get us back to where this had initially been leading. "You're not seeing anyone right now?" I only asked out of curiosity. No other reason.

"Nope. I...this is kind of embarrassing, but after that

week with you, I shut down on that front completely. Not in a bad way. It was just a really good week, you know? And I wanted to take some time to reflect on it and hold it so it didn't disappear into time the way things do. Then there was so much to do to get ready for graduation. My portfolio became my priority. Then finding a job. And then getting ready to move. And now...well, it dawned on me recently that there would always be something else to distract me if I let it. So I'm putting myself back on the market. Seriously. I'm not looking for casual. I'm not looking for a pass-the-time kind of fling. I want the next guy to be The One. The universe has always been really good at delivering what I need when I need it, so I'm putting my intention out there, and I'm not settling for anything less."

My body felt heavy. My feet felt nailed to the floor. I hadn't even realized until that moment that I'd been hoping to take her home with me. I'd even choreographed it in my mind, how I'd offer to share a cab. Then invite her to see where I live. Then lead her through my lonely spotless lounge and to my bed where I swear I dreamed about her every night. Then...

Well. That wasn't happening now. Nothing was happening between us.

I'd already known that deep down. Hadn't I?

"Of course waiting for The One also means I'm horny as hell." She tried to hide her blush behind a tilt of her wine glass, but I still saw it.

Oh. That meant..."You haven't had any sex at all since, since...?" I couldn't finish my sentence. I was too flattered, too dazed, too blown over.

"Nope. No one since you. Do you think my hymen has grown back? Is that a thing?" Another round of giggles. "You should see your face! I've never seen someone look so shocked and intrigued all at once."

Now I really wished for another night with her. One where I could spank her ass red for all her teasing.

"I'm sorry," she said, and I wondered what she would have said if she could read my thoughts? Would she have changed her mind about no flings? Would she jump in my lap and purr like the kitten I knew she was? "It's too fun to wind you up. Does that make me a bad person?"

"I don't think so," I said honestly. "Not when I enjoy it so much."

We lingered in the pub, chatting and laughing. We had a second glass of wine each, then coffee (for her) and tea (decaffeinated, for me). By the time we left it was almost nine o'clock. The temperature had dropped, and when we stepped outside, she shivered.

"Would you like to share a cab?" I still hoped for the possibility of ending up in her arms. The only enemy I had here was my own.

She shoved her hands in her pockets and looked down the street that was very much empty of taxis. "It's only a block to the tube. We could be there before a car comes by, I bet. Walk with me?"

I nodded as though I had any choice in the matter, but I didn't. I was a slave to her at this point. I would follow wherever she led as long as she let me.

We walked together, close enough that our arms brushed. I could feel the heat of her all along my right side. I wanted to tuck myself into it. I wanted to live there.

I tried to imagine a different life—one where I'd met her in my twenties, before I'd become jaded and cold. Would we have worked in that scenario?

I didn't know. I didn't have the imagination she did to comprehend such things.

At the station, we paused at the spot where we were meant to part. The energy between us felt thick and charged.

"Are you sure you don't want me to accompany you? It's really not that far out of my way." It was, but I didn't care.

And if she invited me in afterward? It would only make more of a mess of things.

She seemed to have come to the same conclusion. "It's a completely different direction, and I'm good on my own."

"You know the route to take? You only travel on this train until Embankment and then switch lines."

"Yes, Dad. I know."

Dad. For once I wasn't sure I liked the term. It put me in a box I didn't like being in, even if it was exactly where I belonged.

"Look," she said, drawing my eyes once more to hers. "I'm not going to pretend I don't want to sleep with you."

I could hear the blood woosh in my ears. I could feel the *but* at the end of her sentence. I held my breath and waited for her to say it.

"But..." There it was. "Since we both have different goals right now, I think it would just make things complicated."

She was so much smarter than I was. So much more mature.

"Very wise," I said.

"Friends?"

"Most definitely."

We shared phone numbers and then, once again, I watched her go.

Friends.

She wanted us to be friends.

Oh, how it pained me to face that, even when I already knew that was all we could ever be. What else did I have to offer her? A few months between the sheets while she worried about her life passing her by? A mostly grown son and a witch of an ex-wife to battle and criticize her?

I wasn't what she wanted. She'd said it clearly.

And even if I was on the same path she was, I couldn't deliver what she needed. She wanted a partner that would be by her side for a lifetime. She wanted a houseful of children. She wanted a picket fence and forever.

Not in my cards. Not anymore.

So we'd be friends.

At least this way I'd still get to have something of her, no matter how small. If it killed me, it would be worth it.

CHAPTER
Five

WE DIDN'T SEE each other for a while after that.
I expected her to reach out. She'd always
been the aggressor in our relationship—whatever our relationship was. Every morning I checked my
phone for texts, for missed calls. Every evening after work,
the same. But there was nothing.

After a few days, I considered contacting her myself.
I'd never been very good about messaging, though, and
I'd only ever used the phone to ring people if I had a solid
reason. While I was comfortable talking to people when I
was around them, coming up with topics out of the blue
was never my strong suit. Not that I didn't have things I
wanted to say to her. There was so much, actually. The tiniest details of my day, especially. The strange man dressed
like a sweet pepper at the underground station. The new
advertisement Creative came up with to sell peanuts. The
snippet of a song I caught on the cabbie's radio. The moments that meant nothing but still made me smile—these
were the things that gave me the urge to pick up my phone
and share with her.

But was that appropriate? Was that what friends did? There wasn't anyone in my life that I did those things with. Did I have no friends?

By Thursday, I was willing to interfere with her so-called kismet. I left work early to walk the banks at St. James's Park, hoping to re-create our union. When I didn't see her, I tried again Friday. I came earlier, I stayed later. Still, no sign of her.

Saturday night crept upon me, and I had a rare gig with the cover band I sometimes played with. We were barely a band, really. We'd been playing together so long now, we didn't need to rehearse. Sometimes Ian would throw in a new song last minute, but it was never too hard to pick up. I played the electric bass. It was an easy instrument, and I could fake most numbers if I didn't know them.

Though we only had shows about once every three or four weeks, playing with Thrashheads was one of the more enjoyable aspects of my life. It was a chance to tune out and relax. A chance to forget about work and teenage sons and ex-wives while I got lost in the chord progressions of the greats—Judas Priest, Metallica, Slayer, Zeppelin.

Saturday's show was in South Belgravia, a section of town that I'm sure Audrey's meme map would call the Decent Pub Dead Zone. The food at the bar was lousy, the service was worse. The crowd, though, was engaged. They were gracious with their applause and sang along to some of the more popular Black Sabbath tunes. It was my kind of gig, my kind of audience. A bunch of old farts born prior to 1979 who still thought old metal was the best kind of rock. Wrinkles and grey hair decorated the faces of almost everyone in the pub, and still I looked for Audrey, as if she'd come to a bar like this. As if she'd stay for a band like ours.

When we were cleaning up, I watched my bandmates with new eyes. We'd played together for almost five years, yet we never went out together. We didn't "hang." I didn't even know where Russell or Dennis lived. I didn't know Clancy's last name, or if Clancy *was* his last name. I didn't know these men at all.

"Are we friends?" I asked Ian, the lead singer and guitarist of the band. Ian wasn't his real name, I knew that. It was Johnny, but he had an eternal hard-on for Deep Purple, and had taken the name of the lead singer in honor.

"Yeah, mate." Ian stared at me as though I'd asked him if Ozzy Osbourne was the best. "What else would we be?"

I shrugged. "People who play together in a band?"

He tilted his head and studied me. "Is there a difference?"

I shook my head, because I didn't know, obviously.

The rest of the weekend passed. Monday arrived, and my phone was still silent. Again I went to the park, this time with an umbrella in hand since the rain had returned. I stood at the water's edge and watched the lake break up with each splash of water, watched the increase of activity as the rain quieted and the fish came up to the surface to eat the worms that had been uncovered in the storm.

I felt like one of those fish, a creature that dwelled in the deep dark, only coming out of my sanctuary when baited. And then, how vulnerable and exposed I was in the translucent shallow water. On exhibition and bare to the elements.

I went home, taking the first taxi I found. I didn't return to look for Audrey at the park again.

Were we friends?

On Tuesday, after the office was closed and almost everyone had gone home but me and Amy, I was still thinking about my social life, or lack thereof. "Do you have any friends?" I asked her.

"Besides you?" Her brow wrinkled and she tugged at a corkscrew curl while she thought about it. "I suppose there's Dante. We work out together. And by work out, I mean we run on the treadmill for five minutes then go back to his house and bang like bunnies."

I frowned. "I don't think that's the definition of friends." If it were, I would've accompanied Audrey home that night, and every night.

"Oh really?" Amy thought for another moment. "What's the point then?"

So I didn't text and I didn't ring because, as Amy said, what was the point? And I tried not to think about Audrey, tried not to let her infiltrate my every waking moment, but it was hopeless. She was a cataract covering the lens of the eye—it was impossible to see the world without seeing her.

Then, Friday came. I took a long time shutting down for the day, a futile attempt to make the workweek last longer. I'd begun to dread the weekends and their dreary monotony. Eventually, the cleaning crew arrived and there was nothing much for me to do.

I put on my suit jacket and checked my mobile phone for the first time since lunch. There was finally a voice message from her.

"Hey, it's Audrey. I'm sorry to call out of the blue like this, but I need you! It's an emergency. Can you call me right away?"

I'd never pressed the RETURN CALL button so fast

in my life. "Audrey! Are you hurt? Are you ill?" I didn't even bother with the greeting, I was so anxious to discover her ailment, so eager to help. "Do you need me to come to you?"

"Dylan! It's you! Thank you for calling back." She didn't sound nearly as exasperated as she'd been in the message. "And I'm fine. It's not that kind of emergency. Sorry to panic you!"

"Then you don't need me after all." I didn't know whether to feel disappointed or relieved.

"No, I *do* need you. It's just not life or death—I have a tendency to be dramatic. But it *is* important. Very important. To me, anyway."

Relieved then. I'd feel relieved. And also, while she chattered on, I couldn't help but remember the last time I'd been on the phone with her, when the thing she needed was of a carnal nature. Would this call go in the same direction? Was I a monster for wishing it would?

"Let me hear it." I leaned back in my chair and loosened my tie.

"First, I'm dreadfully sorry I'm asking this so late, but see, the thing is, the museum is having a fundraiser tomorrow night. It's a big fundraiser, a really important one, and each of us is expected to bring at least one guest who might donate. And there really isn't very many people that I know besides you. There's Lawrence, but I'm afraid his tattoos won't go over so well with my boss, not since he got the ones covering his face, anyway, and Betty said she'd go, but she's homeless. And she looks it. There's no way anyone's going to believe that she could give a dollar to our cause. Er, a pound, I guess it is. And Percy has another obligation, so he doesn't think he'll make it. And I know it's really a big favor to ask, the kind that crosses the line—"

"I'll come," I said, cutting her off. Was there really any other choice?

"You will? You can't know what this means to me. Thank you. Thank you! It's tomorrow, though. Is that going to work? Can you get a tux? I really wouldn't bother with any of this if I didn't think I needed to make a good impression on my boss."

"Yes, I'm free tomorrow night. And I own a tux. I'll be there." Joyfully. With bells on.

She could tell me more about Lawrence and Percy then, though I wasn't sure I wanted to know. Facial tattoos? I shuddered. And who was this homeless Betty person she was milling about with?

"You're free! It's—"

"Don't say it," I warned. I didn't want to hear that K word again. Not after this last week and a half.

"Not saying it doesn't make it any less true," she said coyly. "But fine. I'm glad you're available. It's *convenient*. And thank you again. I can't say it enough. I mean it. I'm overflowing with gratitude. And I don't expect you to donate anything. In fact, please don't. It would be utterly humiliating for me if you thought that I only wanted you as a friend for your cash resources. All I need is someone who *looks* like he'll donate, and you very much do."

Her concern for my pocketbook was adorable. "I can be charitable. Especially to a good cause, such as art."

"No, I mean it, Dylan. I will die. Please."

"All right then," I acquiesced. "I won't even bring my checkbook."

I brought my checkbook.

It seemed rude to show up to such a thing without it, and if the museum needed funding, I was happy to oblige. Because I liked good art, of course. I was often philanthropic with my money. It didn't have to be about Audrey in the least.

We decided to meet at the Gallery, though that hadn't been my first choice. I'd offered to pick her up. I didn't regularly use a hired car when I was home in London, but I did own an automobile that I rarely used, and it wasn't difficult to obtain a driver, even on short notice. But Audrey insisted that I didn't go to the trouble.

So there I was, entering the familiar museum with the exhilaration of a first-timer, knowing soon I'd see the most beautiful works of art in the world.

"May I see your invitation, sir?"

I raised my eyebrows at the door attendant, thrown off by the expectation of something I did not have.

"I...hmm." I stalled as I scanned the room behind him, searching for my "ticket" in. "I'm here as a guest of a member of staff?" I hadn't quite meant it to sound like a question, but I wasn't sure enough to let it be a statement.

"Ah," the gentleman said. He opened the binder in front of him. "Then you'll be on the list."

I opened my mouth to deliver my name, when all of a sudden, there she was, swooping in to my rescue.

"It's okay, Cameron," she said, slipping her arm

through mine. "This is Dylan. He's with me."

My heart stuttered. How long had it been since I'd been *with* somebody? It wasn't as terribly awful as I remembered, hearing her say it now.

Cameron checked off some line in his binder and let us in. Though we walked together, Audrey was the one in the lead, directing me past the crowd of donors that always huddled at the front of these sorts of things into the emptier center of the room.

As always, she prattled as we walked. "It's really busy already. I had no idea there would be so many people here. I've been to a couple of these before—one at the last museum that I interned for in Delaware. That was really nothing like this at all. Half of the guests were in jeans. And there was another for a library museum in Pennsylvania that I happened to get an invitation to. Also not the same. Neither museum really had any art worth funding, for one thing, and even if there was, they weren't the kind of places to draw attention from donors with deep pockets. Here's a good spot to people-watch. Let me look at you."

She stopped suddenly and put her hands up as if to keep me in place while she took two steps backwards. Then she threw her hand over her heart and exclaimed, "Dylan! Swoon!" She actually said the word *swoon*. The lilt in her voice and the way she moved her body put emphasis on the word. "You are absolutely magnificent in a tux," she continued, then bit her bottom lip as if to contain herself from saying more. "I can barely stand it."

She was the magnificent one, dressed again in the deep red gown she'd worn at her sister's wedding.

I told her, too. "And you truly look stunning, Audrey." My tone was light as I said it, not because I didn't mean it, but because she took my breath away. Always. *Always.*

She waved her hand dismissively. "It's super tacky to wear a formal twice, but I figured you're the only one here who would know." She put a finger to her lips. "Shh. Don't tell a soul."

"Not a word."

And I winked. Me—winking. I'd truly lost my head now.

If she noticed, she didn't let on. She took my arm again and perused the crowd around us. "I'll tell you who I know. The list isn't long. That woman, over there, with the sharp features and the brocade top? That's Etta, our marketing consultant. And the man next to her is Silas. He's my supervisor. He's in charge of conserving all the Raphael works. Can you believe that? Raphael! He's personally worked on *St. John of the Baptist Preaching* and the *Mackintosh Madonna*. I was dying just to be in the same room with them, and he got to touch them and look at them under the magnifying glass. Dead, I tell you."

I barely had time to agree before she was drawing me deeper into the museum.

"Over there to the right, the short one with the ridiculously large bosom? That's Sasha. She's an art handler, which is basically a fancy way of saying assistant." She lowered her voice as if the next part was a secret. "She barely makes more than I do, and I'm at the bottom of the heap. Oh, and the guy over there, the one talking to that dorky little guy with the tan suit?"

I looked over at the men. "By 'dorky little guy' you mean the Speaker of the House of Commons?"

She giggled as she blushed. "I just called the Speaker of the House of Commons a dork? I'm so embarrassed."

"Don't be. It's rather accurate."

She stayed pink though. "Well, the Speaker of the House of Commons is talking to Mr. Cavendish. No one knows what Mr. Cavendish does, no one knows what his first name is. He *insists* on being called Mr. Cavendish. I reckon he's really important though, because how can you insist on being called anything otherwise?"

That did seem reasonable. "And also," I added, "he is speaking to one of the most prominent dorks in England."

"Yes," she giggled again at my joke, making my chest feel warm. "That too."

Instantly, she had me in tow again, her eyes searching frantically around the room. "Somewhere around here is Jana. She's my boss. We need her to see us—or you, at least. I think she thought I was making you up when I said I had someone to add to the guest list this morning. It was too late to tell her last night. I have to show her you're not a figment of my imagination. Just, where is she...?"

Audrey was running herself—both of us, actually—in circles. I guessed she was nervous, and why shouldn't she be? It was her first big job, her first big event, and certainly she wanted to make a good impression.

I presumed that would be easier if she were just a touch calmer.

"Excuse me, one second, would you Audrey?" I stepped away before she could stop me, and headed to the nearest waiter. I retrieved two glasses of champagne from his tray, then returned to the girl I had left waiting. "Drink this," I ordered. "You'll feel better. Trust me."

"I'm being a little much, aren't I?" She took a sip, though, as I'd asked.

"Never," I said. Because it was true—she was never much, as far as I was concerned. She was always much *more.*

She didn't look like she necessarily believed me, but she took another sip of the champagne, followed by a deep breath. Then another. And a third. Then she knocked the remainder of the glass back, and smiled brightly. "Better now."

I took a swallow from my own glass so that I wouldn't grin more than was appropriate, although I feared I was already failing.

Since I was already acting like an infatuated dolt, it seemed like the best time to continue making a fool of myself and expose my jealousy. "You've made other friends in London, according to what you said the other day. Good friends, I hope?"

She scrunched her face up as she tried to figure out what I was referring to.

"You mentioned a Percy and a Betty. And Leonard?" It was Lawrence. I hadn't forgotten. I just wanted her to think I had.

"Oh, yes! I've met so many awesome people since I'd gotten here, it's hard to keep them all straight. Betty is amazing. She's this woman who lives on the street between my house and the tube stop. I bring her a sandwich every day." She frowned suddenly. "Except not on the weekends. I didn't even think about the weekends! I have to bring her one tomorrow and apologize for forgetting about today. Maybe I'll bring extras next Friday."

It was both moving and adorable how she felt responsible for this woman, as if she'd adopted her like a stray cat. Her concern for this new friend was an admirable trait, one I definitely didn't possess at her age. I wasn't certain that I possessed it now.

"And Lawrence, not Leonard, is a bartender at the pub down the street from here. He makes the best mixed drinks. I never know the names. I always ask him to surprise me. I mean, I'm not a lush or anything. It's just fun to go out after work every once in a while, even by myself. I like to study the people while I'm unwinding."

I could imagine this. Could picture her, all this time, going to a pub after finishing her job. Times she could've texted me to join her. Times I could have offered to take her to the best pubs in the city. That was something friends did, wasn't it? Was she as awkward at this new relationship label as I was or did she simply never think of inviting me?

"And Percy," she looked away. Purposefully? "He's an artist who lives in my building. He…He likes me, I think. He's asked me out a couple of times, but it's just never happened." Finally, she met my eyes. "But maybe I should take him up on the offer. What do you think?"

I thought she should never be with anyone but me. Because I was selfish and obsessed.

It wasn't fair to her because I didn't want her. Not really. Not the way she wanted to be wanted.

I cleared my throat, and attempted not to be the greedy asshole that I was. "I don't know the man, but you did say you wanted to date. If he's someone that you think could possibly be that special guy…" It was really hard not to cringe as I spoke. "Then I say go for it."

She sighed, and when she spoke she almost sounded disappointed. "You're right. I did say that. I'll think about it."

And I'd think about it too. Much more than I should.

"Oh my word!" she exclaimed suddenly, peering over my shoulder. "Carefully, carefully, look behind you.

Dena—she's another intern. She's as nervous about keeping her job as I am, so she told me she was going to hire an actor to play a rich donor since she doesn't know anybody in town. And oh my gosh, who she hired is fantastically ridiculous."

I turned to look behind me.

"Carefully!" she warned with a hiss. "Don't make it look like you're looking."

I took another swallow of my drink and turned as casually as possible. I saw who she meant immediately. The man wore a traditional tuxedo, complete with a top hat and cane. The mustache he sported was pure white, and if we could see under the hat, I suspected he was balding. He looked like a fraud, like a caricature, an exaggerated imitation of a rich man stereotype.

"He looks like that guy from the Monopoly game," Audrey whispered at my side. "He's only missing the monocle."

He did indeed, but… "Rich Uncle Pennybags does not have a monocle."

"He doesn't?"

"No. That's Mr. Peanut. And also Scrooge McDuck."

"Scrooge McDuck has spectacles," she said defiantly. "And your error about that makes me less likely to believe you about Rich Uncle Pennybags not having a monocle— is that really his name? On the other hand, you *are* very wise. Maybe I should trust you."

"I am wise," I agreed teasingly. "And I know my rich old men."

She put her hand up to straighten my bow tie. "Not so old. Not old at all, really." Her hand lingered on my chest, and I could feel the warmth of it through both the layers of my shirt and my undershirt, all the way to my skin, where it branded like a hot iron. She looked up at me, her gaze trapping mine. Her expression grew serious and intense, and if she kept looking at me like that, staring into me for even one more second, I was going to kiss her.

"You are not going to believe this!" Dena, the woman with the hired date, pulled at Audrey's arm for her attention. "Am I interrupting? I'm so sorry if I am. I just have to talk to Audrey."

Audrey glanced furtively between me and her coworker, apparently torn between the two of us.

"Go ahead. I can entertain myself for a few moments." A minute alone was probably a good idea right about now, anyway. I needed to regroup, gather the wits she always managed to scatter back about me.

She seemed soothed by my permission, her features relaxing. "I'll be right back." She stood on her tippy toes and gave me a peck on the cheek before rushing away with her friend.

I felt the place where her mouth had been for long moments after she walked away.

She hadn't been gone long when I was approached by a brunette with a silver streak in her hair. "Good evening, we haven't met yet. I'm Jana Spruce, the art director here at the Gallery. Are you enjoying yourself this evening?"

Jana—Audrey's boss.

"I am, thank you. It's a lovely event. I'm here at the request of one of your employees, I believe. Audrey Lind. I'm Dylan Locke."

Jana lifted one brow in surprise. "Nice to meet you, Mr. Locke." She shook my hand. Hers were cold and bony, especially compared to Audrey's warm ones.

Already I missed the heat of her.

"I hope you don't mind," Jana said, stepping in closer, "but it *is* my job to try to entice you into a donation. We could use your support, Mr. Locke."

I scanned the room to be sure Audrey wasn't watching—she wasn't—and pulled my checkbook from my inside pocket. "I'm very interested in making a donation. Could you tell me what the money is going for? Specifically?" I started to fill in the check with the details—the Pay To, the date.

"Certainly. We are always in need of funds, of course. Grants and endowments only go so far, I'm afraid. Donations cover daily operations and pay our staff. This particular fundraiser is meant to pay for the renovations we have set for January."

I'd read about these renovations in the paper. "I thought the renovation had already been paid for. Wasn't that part of the promise to the public before going on to the next phase?"

"Indeed, Mr. Locke. You know your facts. It's the details surrounding the renovation that need to be paid for. In particular, we are looking for funding for an artist who will watch over the art while the work is being done. We need a specialist to be sure that there will be no damage done to any of the pieces. We're hoping to give that position to one of our current interns."

In other words, this money could secure Audrey's place at the Gallery.

Naturally, I would donate it. "How much do you need to fill the whole salary?"

"We aren't expecting any one person to donate the

whole amount. Any sum you give will be gratefully accepted."

"How much for the full salary?" Was it wrong to want to keep her here? It might have been, but it was also one thing I could give her when I could give her nothing else.

Jana said an amount that made me blink—an increase to Audrey's current pay, no doubt—but it wasn't too much to put a dent in my checking account. I filled in the total for the entire salary, signed my name, and handed the check over.

"Mr. Locke, I don't know what to say. I'm very appreciative." The way she batted her lashes, it seemed she was interested in more than just the sum I'd given her. She was an attractive woman. And likely born in my generation. Another time, I would have paid more attention to her.

She handed me a business card from her jacket pocket. When she placed it in my hand she left hers there a little too long. "Here's my card, if you need anything."

From the husky texture in her voice, it was clear she meant *anything*.

I took the card and put it in my jacket along with the checkbook.

"Audrey did say that you would be generous," Jana continued, heavy with flirtation. "I had no idea *how* generous."

A memory suddenly occurred to me from deep in the past. Ellen and I, on the verge of divorce. I'd finally noticed her cheating, finally confronted her. In one of our more heated arguments, I had asked, *"If you wanted to be with other men so badly, why did you stay with me?"*

She had looked me directly in the eye and said, *"Because staying with you paid better."*

Long after the love between us had dissipated, her attraction to my money had lived on.

Was this why Audrey had brought me here? She'd asked me not to make a donation, but had that been a ruse? Was the content of my pockets what she cared about most? Had she only kept our status as friends because it *paid better*?

My throat suddenly felt dry and my skin cold. I looked to where Audrey had disappeared, and found her there again, giggling with Dena. It felt like they were watching me. Had I just walked into the trap they'd set? Willingly, no less.

I swallowed past the desert in my mouth. "Jana—may I call you Jana?"

"Of course."

"I prefer that my donation remain anonymous, even to Audrey." *Especially* to Audrey. I didn't need to bear the humiliation of her knowing I was such a fool over her.

Jana agreed and excused herself to mingle with other guests.

I turned back to Audrey and found her eyes were now glued to something else, some*one* else—a man who had to be around her age, wearing a hideous tux and crossing the room toward her.

She ran up to hug him, exclaiming his name loud enough for me to hear from where I was standing. "Percy!"

I could see things clearly now. Percy, the artist, was the type of man she wanted. A man who saw the world in full color like she did, young enough to give her a gaggle of babies, bold enough to show up at highbrow events wearing a purple suede tux. He likely couldn't pay to take her to a concert or an opera, but he could give her art in the ways that mattered most to her, on paper, in clay. He was the kind of man she could pine for.

And where did I fit in?

Now that I'd paid for her living, I didn't fit anywhere at all. What other interest would a girl like her have in a guy like me?

In quick strides, I approached her, wishing I was a different kind of man—a man who made grand gestures and dreamed big dreams—but I could only be who I was. A middle-aged pessimist who longed for someone out of reach.

"Dylan, this is—" she began when she saw me, but I didn't let her speak.

"Audrey, something's come up. I have to go. I'm sorry." More sorry than she could ever know.

She frowned. "Are you sure? I can come with you!"

"No, you stay." I left before she could say more, before she could change my mind. Before I could once again be sucked into the fantasy of her.

I didn't belong in her world. She didn't belong in mine. Life after love was a desert. That was where I lived. That was my truth. Any vision I had of Audrey being there with me was a mirage.

CHAPTER
Six

"BUT I DON'T get why I can't say it," Aaron said in that godawful whining tone that made me want to claw my eyes out of their sockets.

We were talking over FaceTime. I usually preferred to converse over the phone where he couldn't try to interpret every gesture of mine. I also preferred these calls to take place while I was at home, not at the office, but he'd wanted to show me the art piece he'd drawn for class before he took it to school. His drawing was phenomenal, far superior to anything I could have drawn (he'd definitely gotten his talent from his mother's side), but as often happened these days, our conversation had turned from a complimentary discussion on his shading techniques to a battle about how to speak to adults.

"Because it's disrespectful. You shouldn't call anyone a 'loser,' let alone your own father." I fought the urge to pinch the sides of my nose. This shouldn't be something I had to explain to a fourteen-year-old.

"But I was joking!" That blasted whine again. He

threw himself down on his mother's couch—where was she during all of this? She could be helping here. "You don't understand me."

"I do understand you," I said impatiently. "It makes you feel better about yourself to put other people down, but—"

"That's not why I said it! You don't get it. You don't understand my humor, you don't understand my taste in music, you don't understand anything about me. No one understands me."

It was hard to argue with him. I *didn't* understand him. But I *wanted* to. I wanted him to believe I had all the answers and that I knew everything he needed me to know, but I did not, in fact, know anything. I didn't know why calling someone a loser was a "cool" thing. I didn't know why he insisted on turning everything into an argument. I didn't know what it was he wanted from me or what would make him happy or how his mother and I fell apart. I didn't know if she'd ever loved me or if it had always been about my money or if Audrey had used me for the same reason or if I'd assumed the worst, and most infuriating, I didn't know why I couldn't stop thinking about her and the anguished look she'd given me when I'd told her I was leaving Saturday night.

And right now I didn't know what else to say to my son.

It had been so much easier when these disputes could be worked out with a cookie and a cuddle. Where had the time gone?

"Parents never understand. That's, like, a law written in the stars somewhere," Audrey said, and I nearly jumped out of my chair.

"What, how, what?" I stammered. I'd been facing my computer screen and the windows when she'd walked in behind me, so quietly I hadn't noticed. More importantly, she'd come in without anyone telling me.

I leaned back in my chair and peered out my office door, trying to see if Louise, my assistant, was at her desk.

"There was no one there, so I just walked in. I'm sorry I startled you." She was trying not to laugh. "And I shouldn't have interfered. Sorry! I'll talk to you when you're done here."

She started creeping backward, but Aaron stopped her. "Wait! What were you saying?" He was sitting up again, his face filling the screen.

She glanced at me, as if to ask permission.

"By all means." I wasn't doing any good here. Besides, I needed a minute to calm my heart down.

Now that she'd been invited, Audrey had no reservations. She stepped right up to the desk next to me and knelt so he could see her face. "Hi! I'm Audrey. We met once a long time ago, but no worries if you don't remember. I was just saying that you're right—parents don't understand, and they never will. They share your genes, but there's the generation gap, and frankly, adults are so busy stressing over life, they forget to stop and feel their feelings. They think they've felt it all before, so why bother?"

I had to bite my tongue not to defend myself as both an adult and a parent. Honestly, though, she was right, and I wanted to see where she was going.

"So all that sucks," she said empathetically. "But the good news is that there *are* people who understand you. Maybe you haven't met them yet, but your world is small now. Get through high school. Once you get in college or are out doing the things you want to do instead of *have* to do, you're going to find them. Just wait. It's totally going to blow your mind."

"That's what I thought," Aaron said, sounding more upbeat than he had a moment before. He still wore a scowl, but that was his usual look these days. "And I remember you."

She beamed. "I'm in London now! Cool, huh? Working with people who totally get me. It gets better, man. Totally better."

"Awesome. Thanks."

Right. Thanks. Thanks for saying something I should have known to say myself. Thanks for reminding me how completely inadequate and out of touch I was.

"If this has been settled, can we say goodbye and talk later?" My irritation was apparent. I took a deep breath and tried again. "Your picture is fantastic, Aaron. If you don't get an award for it, I'll be very surprised."

"It's just an exhibition. Everyone's showing their work. There's no awards, Dad."

"Well, there should be." Like I said, completely inadequate.

"Can I see?"

I wanted to be annoyed at Audrey for extending the uncomfortable call, but it was also endearing that she'd asked. She didn't have to.

Aaron held up the drawing, a portrait of his mother done in pencil.

"Oh, my! That's incredible! You did that yourself? And you're only fourteen?"

My chest expanded with pride. "It's quite good, isn't

it? She knows her stuff, too, Aaron. Audrey works at The National Gallery."

"My portraits were never this detailed," she said, dismissing the attention I'd brought to her. "You're really good. You have passion for it, and it shows. That's not something you can teach. Keep it up!"

I heard Ellen calling Aaron in the background, and I wasn't in the mood to explain who Audrey was to my ex. "Yes, keep it up. Best get on to school now. I love you, and I'll talk to you later."

He rolled his eyes at my declaration of affection but said it back, quickly, then ended the call. *Well, that turned out quite better than it could have.*

Thanks to Audrey.

I turned my head toward her. "How did you do that?" And could she teach me?

"Do what?"

"Talk to him without him transforming into a Gremlin."

She blew it off. "It's easier to listen to someone who isn't his parent."

That wasn't all of it. "I wouldn't have even known what to say. I mean, I *didn't* know. Everything I said was wrong."

She gave me a gentle smile. "I'm closer to his age, is all. I remember what I wished someone had said to me."

Pointing out our age difference didn't help with my mood.

"I shouldn't have interfered, though. So I understand if it wasn't appreciated."

God, she could read me. Not quite accurately, but she was close, and that was irritating, for some reason.

Also irritating was her presence in general. I had walked away from her. Why was she in my office? And why did I want her presence to mean something? There was nothing *for* it to mean.

I swiveled my chair sharply to face her. "Do you mind telling me what you're doing here?" I could feel my mouth curled down in the same frown my son had worn. Maybe he'd gotten that particular expression from me.

Still on her knees, she sat back on her feet. "I should have called first. That was rude on my part. I just didn't have the idea to come here until my lunch break was about to start, and I don't know. I got so consumed with getting here, I didn't think about it."

Her demeanor was genuinely apologetic, and with the addition of her permanently sunny disposition, I couldn't help but soften. "You came over here on your lunch break?"

"Yep. I'll have to leave to go back in about five minutes or so. Your office is deceivingly farther away from the museum than I'd guessed."

She'd used her lunch break to come see me. I didn't know whether to be suspicious or delighted.

"Was there a reason you came by?" Suspicious it was, then.

"Yeah. I wanted to see if you were okay after you left so quickly on Saturday."

And now I was delighted.

I sat straighter in my chair, leaned forward a little. I could feel the closeness of her. I was the cat and she the fire. I wanted to stretch my paws out in her warmth.

She seemed to sit up taller as well, stretching toward me. "I didn't even get to thank you for coming."

"You did. I'm sure of it."

"Not properly."

The heaviness of her tone and the innocent way she looked up at me through her lashes had the unfortunate effect of making me think dirty thoughts. Very dirty thoughts. She was on her bloody knees, for Christ's sake. *(Don't get hard. Don't get hard.)*

As always, she was oblivious to my struggle. "Jana said she spoke to you, too," she said, "so I got points for your being there—and may I say good job not letting her talk you into a donation. She's very persuasive. Anyway, thank you. For coming. You didn't have to, and it really meant a lot."

I bobbed my head in a nod, not quite sure how else to respond. Had she really not wanted me there for my money? Had I jumped to conclusions? I could ask, but I was chicken.

"It was nothing. Really." *Bawk bawk.* Such a coward. "I must admit, I did give a small donation. Nothing to boast about."

"Your heart's too soft," she said, then we both laughed because it was me we were talking about. "You're okay, though? What drew you away wasn't too serious?"

"Not too serious at all." She wanted to know, and I felt bad lying to her, but what else could I say? I certainly couldn't tell her I'd run off because I'd felt used, not when she'd never asked for the money. When she'd specifically asked me not to give anything at all.

"Glad to hear it." She stood up and pulled her phone from her pocket. "I've got to be getting back now. Oh, I almost forgot the other reason I came over—want to join me and a few friends for a drink later? We're meeting at a pub down by the park at six."

The pub that Lawrence works at? I had no right to wonder.

"I don't know…" I shouldn't say yes to her invitation. It would only encourage the strange obsession I had for the girl.

"Nope. You can't say no. You left me early on Saturday, and now you owe me a night."

"You're saying I owe you for leaving early when I'd only come as a favor in the first place?" I shouldn't tease her. It wasn't good for my head.

"Yep. That's exactly what I'm saying." She reached out and pulled on my tie. That wasn't good for my head either. Nor the situation in my trousers.

She had to get out of here. She had to leave, before I did something foolish like pull her into my lap.

"I'll go," I said, anything to get her out of my office before she looked down at my growing problem.

"Yay! I can't wait!" She bent down to press a quick peck on my cheek—a habit that was surely meant to drive me mad. "I'll text you the address. Gotta go. See you then!"

I called after her. "Audrey, Jana doesn't hold a candle to you. You're the one, it seems, who's very persuasive."

She shrugged innocently. "Why do you think I had to come in person? I knew you'd have a harder time turning me down." She waved, opening her hand and closing it the way Aaron had when he was little. Then she disappeared down the hall.

My sigh was audible in the now quiet room.

Maybe she didn't mean to have me wrapped around her little finger, but I was. I so very much was.

It only took half an hour to decide that twenty-somethings were too loud.

The pub was full of them, baby-faced Millennials with more energy at dinnertime than I had at six in the morning. The most raucous sat at our table. I couldn't name them all, even after being introduced. Dena, I remembered, from meeting her at Saturday's event. The rest I gave descriptors to in my head like they were Stieg Larsson novels in order to keep them straight. The Boy with the Nose Ring. The Girl with the Hyena Laugh. The Girl with the Cat Hair. The Girl without a Uterus—I'd learned that within moments of meeting her. Twenty-somethings were also very open, it appeared.

Then there was me—The Man Who Didn't Fit In.

It didn't take a genius to see that I was out of place and sinking quickly. I didn't share their exuberance, I didn't like their music, I definitely didn't know their lingo. In many ways it felt like the conversation with my son, except worse, because I didn't have authority over any of them and because I loved my son.

The only one I cared for at this gathering was Audrey.

At first, I tried to connect—I really did. I inquired about their jobs—they all worked together at the museum. I asked about their hobbies. I answered every question about the advertising business and squashed every ridiculous notion they had about PR people. I didn't know how to keep any conversation going, though. Every one crashed and burned after only a handful of volleys.

After one particular exchange that ended with The Girl with the Cat Hair telling me to "check my privilege," I resolved to keep my mouth shut except to give short, polite answers when addressed and to drink my wine.

Audrey attempted to make the whole thing bearable. "You aren't having any fun," she said with a pout, while the others argued about the ending to the latest comic book turned movie.

"I'm fine," I reassured her. "I never have fun."

She smiled, keeping her gaze steady on me. "That's not true. We've had fun together."

Yes. Yes, we had.

Dena pulled at Audrey's arm, demanding her attention. "Remember when Trevor told Jana that he couldn't get it up? When he was talking about mounting the Manet? Did you see Jana's face?"

Trevor. That was The Boy with the Nose Ring's name.

Audrey broke into laughter with the others. "She went five shades of red, didn't she?" With her focus still on the others, she rested her hand on my lower thigh as though it would have no effect on me. As though I wasn't a functional man made of flesh and blood and sexual desire.

Or maybe as though I was exactly that.

I remembered her words when we'd parted that first night—*I'm not going to pretend I don't want to sleep with you...* Did she still mean that? It was pathetic how much I wanted her to mean it, even if it could never go anywhere. At least, then, she'd be as miserable as I was fighting my lust in her company.

As miserable as I was right now, trying to ignore the

casual sweep of her thumb back and forth over my leg. My cock twitched, wondering if it should get involved.

The answer was no, it shouldn't.

I went to the bar to order another glass of wine.

"At least the fundraiser went well," The Girl without a Uterus was saying when I returned. "I heard Mr. Cavendish say they raised enough to hire two employees full-time after Christmas. Trevor's guaranteed one of them. Must be nice having a set of balls."

Trevor glared at her. "It's based on seniority. You know that."

"It should be based on talent," someone else said, I didn't pay attention who. I was too consumed with wanting to be sure that Audrey had the other job, the job I'd paid for her to have.

"Who's getting the other position?" After so long remaining silent, it felt like all eyes were on me.

Dena answered first. "Don't know yet. Audrey and I are the only other two interns. We were hired at the same time, so it's up in the air, for now. Me and my girl are going to have to duke it out, and by duke it out I mean sit back quietly with our hands tied while someone else decides our fate."

Fan-fucking-tastic. I'd given over a check, felt used in the process, and the money might not even go to the woman I meant it for.

I looked over at her, at Audrey, and found her staring into her beer mug. The pressure to perform must feel overwhelming.

"I'm sure you'll get it," I said quietly when the others had moved on to a new topic. She would, too, even if I had to contact that Jana and threaten to cancel my check.

"Thank you for the vote of confidence." She gave me a smile that quickly vanished. "I'm still not sure I want to stay in London, though."

It felt like I'd been socked in the gut. Like all the air inside me had been knocked out of my lungs, like I couldn't get a breath in. I'd assumed a job offer would be all she'd need after stating she was mainly focused on her career at this time in her life.

But she'd also said she wanted to settle down. With The One.

It was impossible to know what to wish for now. I wanted her here, because I was obviously enjoying being tortured with her presence. But was I so much of a sadist that I wanted to watch her fall into the arms of another man?

Thinking about it made me uncomfortable. Being near her made me antsy. I excused myself and took my wine to wander around the pub. When I found an unused billiards table, I took off my jacket, racked up, and practiced sinking shots.

This was better than being with Audrey and her friends. Reading the table, calculating sides, these things took logic and focus and skill. I didn't have to think about what I wanted or what she wanted. There were no feelings in pool.

I wished there were no feelings in my life.

Blue stripe to the left side pocket.

But I really didn't, did I? Because I liked the feeling I'd had when Audrey showed up at my office. I liked the feeling I'd had when she encouraged my son. I especially liked the feeling I had when she kissed my cheek or placed her hand on my thigh.

She made me feel good in so many ways.

Yellow stripe to the left side pocket.

But she'd also made me feel bad. She had the power to do it again, and I knew it. Which was why I'd decided to stay away from her.

So why was it I'd agreed to come out with her tonight?

Green to the corner.

The ball sank cleanly in the pocket.

"That was crazy! How did you do that?"

I didn't need to look up to know the praise came from Audrey, but I did anyway. Because I liked looking at her. "How did I do what?"

"Shoot the ball like that. So it would swerve to go into the pocket."

A complicated question, trying to reduce years of skill into a simple instructional paragraph. I doubted my usual "geometry" explanation would work on an artist. I ran my hand through my hair before I made the attempt.

"It's all in how you hit the cue ball. If you give it spin on the left, it's going to move right. And vice versa. Then add speed and pressure, and of course, the distance between the cue ball and the other ball has to be taken into consideration." I lined up my next shot. "Red, corner pocket," I announced before squirting the ball and sinking it in.

"That! How did you do that? And how did you make sure the cue ball didn't follow it in?"

I chalked up while I studied her. "Have you never played pool?"

"A bit. It didn't look exactly like this. The balls were

bigger." She giggled at the word *balls*. "Sorry. I have the maturity level of a middle-schooler."

The maturity level of my son. This was why she got on with him so well.

Speaking of low maturity levels... "Where are the others?"

"They all left. It's just you and me now."

Time for me to be leaving too, in other words. If I knew what was good for me.

"So you going to teach me how to hit the ball like that?"

Or I could do that.

I cleared my throat. "We can do this another time. If you'd rather be going." God, I was obvious. Practically begging her to validate my being here.

"Nope. I wouldn't rather." She stepped closer and pulled on the knot in my tie, loosening it from my neck. "I'm sorry they're so obnoxious. I like them. I mean, they're my only friends here, really. Besides you. But they're kind of shallow."

"No, no. I wouldn't say that." Only because I was polite.

"They are. You don't have to defend them. I'm saying it because I want you to know that I hope you don't see me as that shallow. The gossip and unwinding is fun on occasion, but it gets old. And I want more from my personal relationships than that."

I wanted more details. I wanted to know exactly what she wanted from her relationships, and then I wanted to be the one to give her those things.

But she was standing too near to me, and I couldn't think right. So all I said was, "Okay."

She smiled softly. A beat passed, where we just stared at each other. The air crackled around us.

"Like pool!" she exclaimed suddenly, pulling my tie from my neck and breaking the tension with her exuberance. She wadded up my tie and dropped it in my hand. "Teach me how to do that shot."

It was a terrible idea, and I knew it. I didn't have to play through the possibilities of what might occur if I stayed to know that all of them would end in me kissing the fuck out of her, if I had my way. Friends. Sure, we could be friends, but I wanted to be a certain kind of friend. The kind allowed to touch her and caress her and make her come.

I think it would just make things complicated.

That's what she'd said that first night in London. It played over and over in my head, a taunting reminder why I couldn't have the things I wanted. Because I was a decent man. Because I'd lived long enough to know those complications weren't simply excused.

I was wiser and more experienced, and I *knew*. That was why I should go.

And yet I couldn't help myself where Audrey was concerned.

I stuffed the tie in my trouser pocket and picked up the white cue ball, memorizing approximately where it sat on the current table. "Here's what you see when you're aiming. Pretend there are eight points around the circle and one in the middle." I pointed at the top point and then circled clockwise as I named the positions. "Straight follow-through, follow-through with squirt to the left, squirt to the left where the ball stops, squirt to the left and the ball drops back." I repeated the positions on the other side. "Hit straight in the center for no sidespin and no follow."

Her eyes glazed over. "I didn't get a single word you just said."

I chuckled. I'd never been the best of teachers. "It will be easier if I show you." I placed the cue ball back where it had been. "Come here," I said, tugging her in front of me. "What shot would you take?"

I could smell her, the faint whiff of apple in her hair, the sweet natural musk of her body. While she studied the table, I closed my eyes and breathed her in.

"I'd probably go for the orange, because that's close to a straight shot. But I wouldn't know how to hit it so that the white ball wouldn't follow."

I opened my eyes and surveyed her options. It was a solid choice. I handed her the stick. "Let's line it up."

She bent over the table. I wrapped my arms around her so I could help guide the tip.

Or maybe I simply wanted the excuse to touch her. Cartainly if Trevor, The Boy with the Nose Ring, had asked me to teach him, I wouldn't have used this hands-on technique.

"You want it to swerve to the right, and you don't want the cue to follow." My mouth was at her ear. I could feel her breaths become shallow, matching up with mine. Was her heart racing like mine was too? "To get the squirt right, we're going to hit the left side of the cue. Because we want it to draw back when it hits the orange, we're going to aim down."

"So I'm going to hit the tip on the lower, left side of the white ball." Her tongue swept over her lower lip, and my dick went stiff.

"That's correct." I closed my eyes again, and a memory overtook me. Not a memory, actually, but I suddenly remembered what it felt like to believe in wishes. Remembered what it felt like to put my intentions out into the universe and believe there was a possibility they would come true.

I wished right then that this moment would never end, that I could hold Audrey in my arms indefinitely.

When I opened my eyes, she was looking, not at the ball, but back at me. Her face was within centimeters from mine. Her lips were right there, begging to be plumped and bruised with my kiss. I just had to lean forward. She just had to stretch back.

I didn't breathe.

"Why did you leave on Saturday?" she whispered, her gaze never leaving my mouth.

"Why did you invite me tonight?"

"I asked first."

Her tiger eyes were heavy and dilated, her body soft in mine. She wore her desire openly. Blatantly. I would only have to close my pelvis against her ass, and she'd know how much I wanted her as well. I didn't even have to answer the question. I could just kiss her, and I was certain she'd be mine with no resistance.

But mine for how long?

Mine for a night, and then what? At what point would she remember the things she planned for her life were incongruent with the things ahead in mine? If I was this attached to her now, how attached would I be to her then?

I'd lived through heartache before. I wasn't subjecting either of us to that pain.

I stood back, letting go of her, the pool shot long forgotten. "I left so that I wouldn't be a third wheel," I lied, and yet, hadn't that been true too? "Your friend, Percy, had arrived. You've clearly indicated you're looking for a romantic relationship right now. I didn't want to stand in the way of an opportunity."

She straightened but didn't look at me. "Oh. That was very thoughtful."

I didn't imagine how disappointed she sounded. How hurt.

I hated myself in the moment. Not for what I'd done, because it was better to let her go like this. Better to encourage her on the road to whatever happiness existed on her path—hopefully there was more for her than there had been for me.

No, I hated myself for being the one who had to teach her this lesson, that life wasn't all roses and rainbows. That it was unwise to indulge every passing fancy. That sometimes it was better to be injured in the battle instead of killed in the war.

She dropped the cue stick and turned toward me, an overly bright grin on her face. "I really should go out with him. I've been procrastinating for no reason at all. In fact, I would like to call it a night, if that's okay with you. Maybe I can stop by his place and see him before it gets too late."

I already had second thoughts, already regretted sending her into the arms of a man who was most likely better suited to her than I ever could be. Already regretted not taking one more kiss.

She was good enough to hurry and be gone before I had a chance to do anything about it.

CHAPTER
Seven

AUDREY: Percy is a terrible kisser.

I was in my kitchen, heating up the casserole my housekeeper had left in the freezer for me when my phone buzzed with the text. After three days of not hearing from Audrey—three days of managing not to reach out myself—that was the last message I'd expected to receive.

I didn't want to know the details.

But I also did. Especially if they were terrible.

Except, what if there was more than just kissing? The thought of Audrey in any man's arms was near impossible to bear. I didn't want to know. I Did. Not. Want. To. Know.

DYLAN: You kissed Percy?

I had no will, obviously. No restraint in the least.

AUDREY: Yes, and it was the worst. I can't possibly go out with him.

I leaned against the counter and gave in. I would need to know everything about how Percy was not the right man for her after all.

DYLAN: You had a date tonight, I presume. Was all of it a disaster? Or just the kissing?

My bets were on the whole thing being terrible. A woman would give a man a second chance after a bad kiss if the rest of the night had been pleasing.

As soon as my phone showed that the text had been received, it began to ring.

I answered just as fast.

"It wasn't actually a date," she said, skipping any formal greeting, as usual. "We bumped into each other in the apartment foyer. I had groceries, so he offered to carry them up."

He'd carried her groceries. That was commendable enough. Not that I was keeping a tally of his good and bad points.

"Then, after he helped me put them away—"

"He helped put the groceries away as well as carried them up?" More commendable than I'd credited him for.

"There weren't that many. A few bags worth. But, yes. And I thought I should offer to make him dinner for going to the trouble, except I didn't want him in my apartment that long. He might get the wrong idea."

A woman making him dinner, alone, in her apartment—yes, he would very much get the wrong idea, if I knew men. And I felt like I had a pretty good handle on the gender.

"So I said, 'Hey, want to grab something at the café?' It's this restaurant just down the street, and I go there all the time when I don't feel like cooking. Which is a lot."

"So you had dinner together. Or he tried to skip dinner all together and kissed you after the groceries?" These facts mattered, as far as I was concerned. Mattered very much.

"We went to dinner. The kiss came later."

"Hmm." I was done giving him points until I heard the whole story. "Go on."

"Dinner was fine enough. He sure likes to talk about himself, though. Every time I tried to bring up another subject, we somehow ended up back on his art. And get this— he wanted to know if I could hook him up with a gallery since I have 'connections.' His word, not mine."

That bastard. No points at all for him. He was negative points now. Minus fifty.

Also, what was Audrey thinking? "He said that to you and you still let him kiss you?"

"Well, you know. I hadn't _planned_ it. Actually, when he walked me to my door, I think he thought I'd let him in for more."

"But you didn't, did you?" I felt like a father, waiting for an answer that might lead to punishment, and I was already revved up to dole it out.

"I didn't."

I practically sighed from relief. "Good girl," I said. The timer went off. I put the phone down on the counter and hit speaker so I could grab the mitts and pull the casserole dish out of the oven without missing a single word of Audrey's story.

"I specifically turned around to face him before opening my door. I thanked him for helping me with the groceries again, and then I said good night. That's when he kissed me."

I couldn't help picturing it—Audrey, with her back against her door, trying to be polite, the self-absorbed Percy leaning in to take her mouth. The image wound me up so tight I almost dropped the baking dish.

"Did you give him any indication you wanted to be kissed?"

"I didn't mean to if I did. How do you let a guy know you want to be kissed?"

"I don't know." I put the food on a hot plate and retrieved the phone. "You tilt your chin up. You lick your lips. You bat your lashes."

"I sort of just smiled. Is that an invitation?" She was wise beyond her years, yet every now and then, her naivety surprised me.

It was like she needed me. Needed me to guide her in these matters so that she didn't get taken advantage of. So that she didn't end up making a mistake she'd live to regret.

"That is most certainly not an invitation if you didn't mean it to be," I lectured.

"I didn't mean it to be, but it's for the best, really. Now I know I don't want to go out with him at all."

"Because the kiss was terrible." I wanted to hear her confirm this one more time.

"Because it was beyond terrible. It was like he thought he'd win a prize if his tongue made it to my tonsils. So he tried several times."

"Ew." How could anyone kiss her like that? Like they were playing tonsil hockey? She was sweet and delectable. She had to be tasted and savored. Her lips were meant to be adored.

"Total ew. Definitely not The One."

I felt good about the phone call, and even better about her conclusion about Percy. Still, I thought she needed a stern reminder about a woman's rights. "Next time a guy tries to kiss you, if you aren't into it, you can turn your head away. You should never be expected to give a kiss just because a man wants it."

"Got it."

"Promise me you'll respect yourself in the future." I was asking for a vow she didn't owe me. Hopefully she thought she owed it enough to herself to give it.

"Yes, Daddy," she said, causing my cock to stand at attention. "Don't let your dinner get cold."

She hung up then, but dinner was still lukewarm by the time I got to it. Taking a moment to rub one out while thinking about Audrey calling me Daddy was definitely worth it.

I received another concerning text from her the next night around the same time.

AUDREY: Is this outfit 2 revealing for a 1st date?

An image of Audrey in a sexy, sequined, low-cut jump-suit accompanied the text.

Yes. The answer was definitely yes.

I had to count to five before I responded. There were too many things I wanted to say, and if I rushed to say it all, I feared I'd say something I didn't mean.

DYLAN: I suppose it depends on the sort of impression you want to give.

There. That was diplomatic.

AUDREY: Never mind. I don't have a jacket that goes with it, and it's 2 cold 2 go without

It was mid-October now. I never thought I'd be so grateful for jumper weather.

DYLAN: Perhaps you have a polo neck? You could pair it with jeans.

Too obvious?

Perhaps. Two minutes passed, and she hadn't responded. I sent another text.

DYLAN: Are you giving Percy another shot after all?

I was suddenly a praying man. Please, oh, please let her answer be no.

AUDREY: No.

Thank God.

Another text followed right away.

AUDREY: Joshua.

Who the fuck is Joshua? I sent another text asking just that. Minus the cursing, of course. I didn't want to seem so invested in the conversation that I required expletives.

This time, her reply came through FaceTime.

Shit. I looked like shit. I'd hit the gym after work and hadn't yet made it to the shower. I'd just peeled off my shirt when she'd texted, and here I was, in gloriously sweaty flesh.

I carefully angled my phone to only see my head and answered the call.

Her face came through the screen, clear and beautiful and innocent. "I met him this morning at the Gallery shop. He asked me out for tonight, and I had no plans, so I said why not."

Now that we'd involved cameras, there was no way she couldn't see my distress. "You can't just go on a date with a stranger! You know nothing about this guy. What if he's planning to kidnap you and sell you into the sex trade business?"

"I'm meeting him in a public place, and I don't intend to go anywhere else with him," she said reassuringly. "And I've told you where I'm going. If I don't call you back by nine, you can send the police. Oh! Dylan muscles. How did I get so lucky?"

I'd inadvertently let the phone slip to show my bare torso. "I was just getting in the shower," I said defensively. But I liked the way she ogled me through the screen too much to correct the camera's view.

"Ooo. Can I join you?"

I blinked. "Pardon me?"

"Kidding!" Though it hadn't sounded like she'd been

kidding. "I'll let you get to it. But first can you tell me if this outfit is better?" She turned the phone so I could see her entire image in a full-length mirror.

The new outfit was not at all revealing. Her pink jumper was indeed a polo neck. but it hugged her breasts and hips and flared out at her wrists in such a sweet feminine way, a way that made her appear as irresistible as she'd appeared in the low-cut jumpsuit. More so, even. I didn't want to encourage her to woo a man in what she was wearing. No man in his right mind would refuse.

But there was no valid reason to object.

"You're beautiful. Beautifully perfect," I said, somberly. "Call me when you're home. I'll need to know that you've arrived safely."

"Thank you. I will. Enjoy your shower." She blew a kiss and was gone.

I didn't enjoy it at all. I didn't enjoy a single moment of the next two and a half hours, waiting for her to ring and tell me she was all right. Not just that she was all right, but that her date had been meaningless and uneventful and that absolutely no kissing had taken place.

Then, when she did ring and tell me exactly that—that Joshua was a "snoozefest with Mommy issues"—I was so relieved that I couldn't let her go without hearing every detail. Then every detail of her day. Then every detail of the past week.

And thus began the new version of our friendship. Our FaceTime friendship.

At first, her calls were much of the same, asking advice about her upcoming date, but she'd always ring again afterward to tell me how awful the night had been before going into the rest of the day's events. Soon she began calling even when she didn't have a date. And when we'd run out of things to say, we didn't hang up, we just sat on the phone together, going on about our evening. Often, we'd even watch a show together.

"I think she used to like the other guy," she said one Tuesday, early in November. "The one who's not her husband. That's why he's acting so weird about it."

It was late, and I'd brought my laptop to bed. Audrey was also in her bed. I had a profile view of her painting her toenails while she watched her show in a separate window on her tablet.

I looked up from my computer, where I was simultaneously FaceTiming with Audrey and working up a spreadsheet for a new campaign, and stared at the telly. We were watching *Easy* on Netflix, and most of this particular episode was in subtitles. I hadn't been paying attention, so I was faking it when I pretended I knew what was going on. "She's going to cheat on her husband."

The show was an anthology type, vignettes from the lives of different characters in Chicago while they fumbled their way through love and other relationships. I'd predicted when we'd started the show that none of them would end up happy.

She scowled. "You say that every episode. Not a one has cheated so far."

"It might not happen in the show, but it would happen if it were real life. Love never ends well. I know you feel differently, but I'd be remiss if I neglected to remind you I've learned otherwise."

"This show makes you miserable, doesn't it? All the people surviving their relationships." She looked directly at me through the screen. "Would you rather we go back to watching *Gogglebox*?"

"No. Please, never again." That show's concept was by far the most dreadful—regular people were filmed in their own homes watching popular British TV. It was one of Audrey's favorites, though, and while I protested about watching it, I quite delighted in watching her laugh through every episode.

I quite delighted in watching Audrey do anything, it seemed. I certainly didn't participate in these calls for the television viewing.

I watched now as she stretched out her legs in front of her, her toenails displaying a bright orange hue. Though I'd thought I preferred lighter polish colors on women, I found I very much liked this shade on her, and I said so.

We settled into a comfortable silence while she watched more of the show, and I filled in more boxes on my spreadsheets.

"Oh my!" she suddenly exclaimed, out of nowhere.

I didn't bother to look up from my work. "What is it?"

"You were right. She *is* cheating on her husband." She let out a hiss of air. "And it's...wow."

That got my attention.

I looked up at the screen, and sure enough, the man who was not the woman's husband was seducing her. In her own apartment. While her husband slept in the next room.

I felt the familiar jumble of rage building in my chest, the righteous anger of a once scorned husband, ready to unleash in a spew of curse words and another rant on Why Love Fails.

Except, I was too caught up in the action on the screen

to go there. Not just my telly screen, but my computer screen—Audrey was mesmerized.

She blinked several times, her hand stroking her skin at her throat. "This is really, super...wrong, of course, but also it's..."

The man had the woman pressed up against the window, going at her from behind. There were plenty of words that could easily be filled in where Audrey left off. *Dirty, filthy, nasty, arousing.*

I chose the simplest. "It's hot," I said clearly. Really hot. So hot, my boxers were starting to feel uncomfortable.

"I miss that," Audrey said in a raw tone. "I mean, I'm really happy with my decision to take this dating thing slowly, don't get me wrong. I have no intention of going to bed with any guy before I'm in a committed loving relationship. But..."

The words *don't get me wrong* were intriguing enough to draw me from the telly screen. No one says *don't get me wrong* without following with a controversial statement.

"But?" I was bracing now for whatever that controversial statement might be. Coming from Audrey, it could be anything.

"But I just have to say, I'm really missing the bedroom action. It's almost been a year since I...well, you know. You were there."

I was as dazzled about this confession as I was the first time she'd told me. I hadn't slept with anyone since then either, not that I intended to confess that to her.

"I think about it sometimes. I think about you and me and how good we were together and sometimes it seems a shame that we only have memories to replay."

"You think about us?" I asked cautiously. As though it didn't matter to me in the slightest what her answer was. As though I didn't bash the bishop nightly after we got off the phone.

"I do. Of course I do. And I know we can't actually do anything because we have completely different philosophies about how romance works, but... Do you know what a buddy booth is?" She was excellent at switching gears mid-topic. Sometimes it was a challenge to follow, but always a fascinating journey, and she generally made it back around to where she started. Eventually.

"I can't say that I do," I said, praying this was one of those times she circled back to the beginning.

"I've never been to one in person, but when I was still in Colorado getting my bachelor's, one of my friends told me about these booths they used to have at the porn shops on Colfax. You'd go in this booth, so small it just had a bench and a TV screen. You'd put your money in and then you could pick a porn movie to watch while you, you know. Did your thing."

I turned off the TELLY. Nothing in the show was as good as this conversation, and I didn't want to miss a single word.

"But there was also a window on the side of the booth, with a curtain. If you opened it, and if the person next to you opened their curtain, you could watch each other. I mean, maybe that's a little gross, depending on who the person is next to you, but if he was normal or if you knew him, it sounded like it could be kind of hot."

"I don't think there are any such booths in London." I didn't know where she was going with this, but if she intended for me to point her in such a direction, I was not about to comply.

"No, I don't want to go to one. They probably aren't even a thing now that the internet is the beautiful place that it is. But I thought maybe. You know. Maybe we could make our own buddy booth. Right here. Over FaceTime."

"Excuse me...what was that?"

"Porn. You and me. We could both turn on a show and—how do you Brits say it? Have a bit of a wank? Our computer screens can be the buddy window. You can watch me. I can watch you. What do you say?"

She was trying to kill me. The only reason we hadn't ended up in bed together already, as far as I was concerned, was because she'd taken it off the table.

And now she was dangling an opportunity to crack one off while watching her do the same?

I was stone hard at the thought.

She had to be pulling my leg, winding me up. Something. She couldn't be serious. So I didn't give an answer.

"Dylan? Dylan. We don't have to if you think it's a bad idea."

"I didn't say that." Most definitely didn't. "I was simply thinking through the possible repercussions."

"I really don't think there are any. We've already had sex. We're still both attracted to each other—I think—"

"We are."

"—and doing it this way will keep things from getting confused. Because it's obviously just a way to get off, and not about anything else. It's going to be fun. You'll see." The view of her changed as she picked up her tablet and set it on her lap. "I'm pulling up a video I have saved. One of my favorites. You should do the same."

The only thing I did on my computer was enable the

image of her to fill the whole screen.

"Okay. I'm playing mine now. Are you ready?"

I wasn't even sure that I'd agreed to this game, but fuck if I wasn't going to play it out. There was no risk that I could see. This wasn't like kissing her—if I kissed her again, I was certain I'd never be able to stop.

Erotic moaning and sounds of kissing played in the background as her video began to play. She put the tablet back on the bed next to her, and the view of her changed again. In profile, I watched as she slid her hand under the waistband of her pajama shorts.

Ah, fuck.

I pushed down my sweats and my boxers, just far enough to release my cock from its imprisonment. There was already lube on my nightstand, and I grabbed it now and applied it liberally to the throbbing steel in my hand.

All the while, my eyes were on her. My ears were tuned to her.

She was breathing heavily while her hand moved inside her shorts. I couldn't see the pink flesh of her cunt, couldn't see if she was still bare or if her lips were glistening with her wetness.

"Are you wet?" I asked, desperate to know.

"I'm so wet."

The moans in the background increased. "What's happening in your video? Describe it to me. In detail."

She turned her head to look toward the screen, her eyes not quite looking at me. "He's going down on her. He's licking her clit, and she's really into it."

I could still taste Audrey's pussy on my lips. Stroking the length of myself, I imagined I was the one eating her out. That I was the one making her make those sounds. Those sweet, sweet cries as she played with herself, stroking herself toward climax.

I bloody needed her pants down. I needed to see her.

"Audrey, be a good girl. Pull down your shorts and let me watch." The words were out before I could decide if they might cross the line.

Fortunately, she didn't bat an eye. Just stripped off her shorts and knickers entirely, tossing them across the bed. Then she spread her legs and moved her screen so that I had a prime view of her gorgeous, pink cunt. Moisture dripped from her entrance. Her clit was swollen and red under her fingers. It was the most erotic thing I'd ever seen. Buddy booths couldn't possibly have been this titillating.

"Put your laptop where I can see you, too, Dylan," she said as she strummed across her sensitive bud, her voice thick.

I set my laptop down immediately, angling the screen so I could see her without turning my head too far.

"There's that monster cock," she said, and I grew even thicker. "What's going on in your video? Tell me what they're doing."

I'd never turned on a porn of my own. The only woman I wanted to watch was the one filling up my screen.

So that was the one I described, giving her directions in the guise of details. "She's alone. She's playing with herself. One hand is squeezing her clit, and with the other, she's pulling on her tit."

Audrey was such a good girl, such a good, good girl. She lifted the tank she was wearing, exposing her round, pert tits. With one hand, she tugged at the tight bead of one nipple, rolling it between her fingers. Lower, she pinched at her clit, harder until her hips were bucking.

The strokes of my hand quickened over my cock. "Now she's putting her fingers inside her. Two of them. She's so wet. She's drenched."

Again, Audrey followed the action of my imaginary porno. Two fingers disappeared inside her. When she pulled them out again, they were dripping with her juices.

"Fuck, that's beautiful." I sat up so I could really watch her when she did it again. And again. And again.

I matched my own rhythm to hers, pretended it was her warm hole I was plunging into instead of the palm of my own hand. I was getting close. I could feel my balls pulling up, could feel the tingling in the base of my spine.

"This isn't enough. I need—hold on." Abruptly, Audrey left the screen for a minute. When she returned, she had a purple dildo.

Jesus.

It wasn't even that big, but it was wider than her fingers. Longer, too. She turned the toy on to vibrate and lined it up to her entrance. If she put that in her tight hole, I was done for.

The truth was, I wanted to be done for.

"Shove it in, now, Audrey. Show me how good you take your fucking." My words were ragged and desperate. And when she shoved it in, I nearly exploded right then. "Ah, that's it. Take it. Put it all the way in. As far as it can go."

She pushed it in until it was deep inside her, then pulled it out halfway before driving it back in. Her tempo was fast, her breathing more shallow with each thrust. Her eyes moved back and forth from her pussy, to the screen—to me or the video, I wasn't sure—but each time I saw them they were more and more glazed over. She was close. As close as I was.

I increased my own speed as I neared the edge. I was out of control, out of my mind. "Does it fill you as good as I can?" I begged for her to answer. "Does it make you feel as good as I do?"

"No," she gasped. "Nothing fills me as good as you do. Nothing."

With those words, I erupted. Cum spilled over my hand as I jerked again and again, slower now, determined to pull every last bit of my orgasm from my cock.

She followed right after, her body spasming with the pleasure of the release. The utter beauty and carnality of the scene urged another wave of my own climax.

I fell back on the bed and tried to remember how to breathe. And figure out what to say. How did a person comment after such an incredibly erotic experience as this?

Audrey was the one who tried first. "That was...I mean...I don't...words." She sat up and reached for her tablet. "I'm trying to say that was good and thank you and all that, but I can't seem to remember how to speak right now, so how about we call it a night and I'll talk to you tomorrow?"

She'd done better conversing than I could have.

"Yeah. Yeah, that's good." The screen went dark when she hung up, but I stared at it for a long time wondering how it was possible that, after all that, I only wanted her more.

CHAPTER
Eight

"WHAT ARE YOU doing? I need you!"

This was a common way for calls with Audrey to begin, as well as my favorite. Saturday when her image came through FaceTime she was dressed in another jumper-and-jeans outfit, half of her hair hidden inside a newsboy cap. She looked delectable. Good enough to eat.

I thought she looked good in everything, though. Especially since the night of the buddy booth. It had been four days since we'd played the game. We'd talked every day since without mentioning what we'd done, but I couldn't stop thinking about it. Couldn't stop thinking about her moan as she came and her erotic confession. *Nothing fills me as good as you do. Nothing.*

Words exchanged during sexual engagement are not to be trusted. I was old enough to have learned that lesson the hard way. Still, I liked the fantasy of it. Enjoyed the fancy of nothing being as good for Audrey as I could be.

At my age, it appeared, a man was still capable of

dreaming.

"What's wrong? Is Jeffrey an asshole?" It was too early for her date to be over. I'd spoken to her while she was getting ready, and she didn't plan to be home until after ten. It was only six-fifteen. I was ready to be mad on her behalf.

"Yes, *Joffrey* is a bad dude. He stood me up."

Thank goodness for him that was all he'd done. I'd never been one to endorse violence, but I'd fight barehanded and without hesitation if it were to defend Audrey's honor in any way. In this case, he was an idiot, but hadn't sparked my fighting instinct.

"Another one bites the dust," I said, perhaps not as conscillatorily as I should have. "Now you can cross him off the list and have your evening free to do as you please. A win-win as far as I'm concerned."

The corners of her mouth turned down into that pout that taunted me so. "Except I'm the one who bought the tickets to the Jack the Ripper tour, and they weren't cheap! Come and join me so they don't go to waste."

"I'm afraid I have other plans."

She rolled her eyes, as obviously as my son did every time we spoke these days. "No, you don't. You never have plans. You're as homebody as they get. The tour doesn't start for an hour, so you have time to throw some real clothes on and get out here."

Real clothes? I glanced down at the outfit I was wearing. They seemed fine to me, but I *was* wearing running pants and trainers. Guess I was changing before leaving the house.

And I *was* leaving the house. Soon, in fact. "I *do* have plans, thank you very much. Seems you don't know as much about me as you think." While I did feel disappointment at not being able to come to her rescue, there was also a sense of satisfaction at not being available. If she ever thought I was waiting around to rush to her aid, now she knew the truth was otherwise.

The truth was otherwise tonight, anyway. I really didn't usually get out for much that wasn't related to work.

She wasn't buying it. "What are they?"

"What are my plans? If you must know, I have a gig tonight." One of the best things about playing with a band was how impressive it sounded to announce that I had a gig. More impressive than our actual music. We were not an original group in any way, shape, or form.

I could practically see her eyes go wide. "You do? You didn't tell me! Forget the Ripper. I'll come to you. Where are you playing?"

Oh dear. That was not at all where I'd planned for this to lead.

I backtracked quickly. "No, you don't want to come to this. It's not your type of music. Barely music at all."

"I don't care how good you are. It's you, and I've been dying to see you play! Thrashheads, right?"

I couldn't believe she remembered. The only time I'd mentioned it had been in passing. "You don't want to see us. I promise. It's going to be a terrible show. Don't ruin your night."

"What time do you go on? What's the address?"

"Audrey, I mean it. Go on the Ripper tour by yourself instead. That will be a much better use of your time."

Her pout had returned, I could hear it, and I prepared myself for another battle round, but she surprised me with her easy acquiescence. "Fine. If you don't want me there…"

I ran my thumb and first finger across my forehead in a pinching motion. "It's not that I *don't* want you there—"

"You just don't want me to see you play. I get it. Whatever. I'll talk to you later."

"Make sure you text me when you're home!" I shouted after her, but she'd already ended the call.

Fantastic.

I'd hurt her feelings. That hadn't been the goal. I considered for a moment, calling her back and inviting her after all, but there were reasons why that wasn't a wise idea. In the end, I deferred to an idiom I lived by—*the more you stir a turd, the more it stinks.*

I decided not to stir the pot.

It was almost two hours later when I heard from her again.

We had thirty minutes before our show started, and I was tuning my bass. The pub tonight near Regents Park was similar to most of the places we played—cheap, old, and empty. The owner of this particular venue was a cousin of a cousin or some equally far-off relation to the drummer, Russell, and the gig was more of a favor to us than to the pub. They didn't feature live music, as a rule, so rather than playing on a stage, the tables and benches in one area of the establishment had been stacked in the corner. We were to perform in front of this precarious tower.

I tuned my bass while Ian and Clancy, our keyboardist, set up their equipment and exchanged digs about the venue. I was doing my best to ignore them, but their sour mood was starting to get under my skin. Why was it we played together, again, if none of us found it any fun anymore? It had been an obligation for so long, I couldn't remember a time that it had been fun at all.

"Holy cow! This is fantastic!"

Oh, God. I knew that enthusiastic voice. It was the last sound I heard before going to bed most nights, the first sound I thought about when I woke up every morning.

With dread, I turned around to face the naughty little vixen. "Audrey," I huffed. "I told you not to come." I was already thinking up excuses to get her out of the place.

They don't allow women. They don't allow women under twenty-five. They don't allow women who know members of the band.

Lame excuses, yes. I'd never been very creative on the spot. And yet I was desperate to paint a picture that didn't include her.

"I'm glad I didn't listen," she said, stepping past the duct tape border on the floor that was meant to distinguish the "stage" from the rest of the pub. "This is, like, a real band, Dylan. With real instruments and real drums."

She used two fingers to do a roll on the cymbal. Russell was going to be livid. No one touched his drums but him.

But I was more concerned about what she'd just said.

"What do you mean this is like a real band? Of course we're a real band. What did you think I meant when I said I was in a band?"

"I don't know." She sat down on the drummer's stool and began thumping the bass drum pedal with her foot. "I guess I pictured more of a bunch of men with microphones and a karaoke machine. Especially when I saw on the map that this place was in the Drunk People Who Missed Camden part of town."

Ba dum da. She'd found the drumsticks now, and her rhythm wasn't that bad.

Russell's voice boomed across the pub. "Who's touching my drums?"

Good. Maybe he'd scare Audrey off.

"How did you find out where I was playing?" I asked, still more focused on the how and the why of her being there.

"Internet. Turns out Thrashheads has a website! A pretty good one, too."

I couldn't help puffing my chest a bit. The website was my doing. "It's more of a Wordpress account, really, but it does..." She was distracting me from the point. The point being I preferred she wasn't here. "Look, Audrey. I can't have you in the audience when I play."

"Will I be very distracting?"

Jesus, she was so adorable sitting behind those drums, her cap tilted on her head, her eyes twinkling with mischief.

Yes, she would be very distracting. She was very distracting already.

"Hey—who are you?" Russell peered down at the woman on his stool, and from his expression, I could tell he was fuming.

"Are you the drummer?" She stood up and handed him his drumsticks. "I've never met a real drummer before. Wow. Look at those biceps. Is that from playing?"

Russell seemed taken aback. "I don't know. A bit, I s'pose."

"That's hot." She gave him that glowing smile of hers, and between that and the compliment, he was won over.

"It *is* hot, isn't it?" He sat down and played through some of his riffs. *Show off.*

"Nice," she said.

Not nice at all. Particularly not nice was the way Russell was looking at her now, like she was the groupie he planned to take home after the set. But she wasn't.

Not on my watch.

"That's enough now, Audrey. Let's go outside and hail you a cab." I put my bass in its stand, but she was right there, ready to pick it back up again.

"Is this what you look like when you play?" she asked, striking a melodramatic pose. She strummed the strings, shifting to a new position with each sour note. "I bet you really get into it when you're onstage."

I didn't know what to say to that. It wasn't very flattering to tell her the truth—that I tended to stand in one place, playing through the chords with precision rather than passion. That I likely looked rather lame in the process. That I didn't remember how to enjoy any of it while it was happening. That I didn't want her to imagine a show that wasn't happening.

"Oh, yeah. Locke really puts on a show," Ian guffawed.

Audrey didn't seem to realize he was being sardonic, or she was protecting me with her response. "Awesome. I can't wait." She pulled the bass strap over her head and handed me my instrument, her fingers brushing mine in the exchange.

I'd forgotten about the power she had over me in real life after only seeing her on screen for the last several weeks. I'd forgotten the way the air vibrated around her, forgotten how she made my skin tingle and my mouth feel dry.

I'd forgotten how much I utterly liked being in her presence.

"I'm so glad my date bailed on me so I could be here. It's kismet, you know."

There she was with that whole thing again. "I'm beginning to think that word doesn't mean what you think it means."

"Oh, I know what it means. Your hair needs mussing. It's too perfect." She reached out to run her hand through the brown flop on the top of my head. My pulse sped up at her touch. "There. Much better."

Our eyes locked. There was something familiar about this, about all of this. About her. About me. Something I couldn't quite put a finger on.

"Are you going to introduce us to your girl, mate?" Ian asked, bringing me back to the present moment.

Your girl. She most definitely wasn't my girl. She was...

"This is Audrey," I said simply. "Audrey, this is Thrashheads. Ian. Russell. Clancy. Bloke flirting with the waitress is Dennis. He plays second guitar."

A chorus of hellos sounded followed by a weighted silence where each of my bandmates looked from me to Audrey questioningly.

For Pete's sake. We knew practically nothing about each other, and now they wanted to know more?

"Audrey is...she's..." I didn't know how to explain Audrey.

"I'm his niece," she said, and everyone let out an audible, *Ah!* Because that made more sense, that she was a relative rather than a friend or a girlfriend. I got it, I truly did. "It's great to meet you all!"

She turned her focus back to me. "I'm going to grab a drink and get a seat before the show starts. Break a leg, and all that. Uncle Dylan." As she often did, she pressed her lips to my cheek.

I'd forgotten how much those kisses drove me out of my mind. Blissfully out of my mind.

"She's a looker," Russell said. "Mind if I—"

"No. Don't even think about it." There was no way in hell Russell was The One she was looking for.

"I thought your brother didn't have any kids," Ian said. Apparently he knew more about me than I remembered.

"She's Ellen's niece. She's living here for a while, working at a gallery. I said I'd show her around." As if I'd bring anyone to a Thrashheads show on purpose.

Which reminded me, I'd wanted her to leave.

I took a step to follow after her and stopped. I didn't actually want her to leave. Not really. I liked that she'd come. I'd only told her I hadn't wanted her to come because I was afraid of looking like a fool. And maybe I still would, but she'd been expecting karaoke, and she'd still bothered to show up. That seemed to indicate that she really didn't care if we were terrible.

So I let her stay.

Then, as the chords started to our first number, and my hand found its position over the frets, I was inspired with the most fascinating notion to let go. Just let go and play. Get my mind out of the way and let my body make the music that I'd loved since I was a teenager.

I got into it. I rocked that bassline. I rocked it on every song. I was brilliant. I was on fire.

I won the nonexistent competition.

It was because of Audrey, of course. She was in the audience, and I wanted to be brilliant for her, so that she wouldn't regret coming. But also, I played good because I *felt* good. Because *she* made me feel good.

She made me feel good the whole night long, the way she cheered and clapped, the way she called out for an encore when we'd reached our last number. The way she sang along to every song she knew. The way she never took her eyes off me.

It was more fun than I'd had in ages.

It wasn't until we were performing our encore piece that it hit me—why all of this seemed so familiar. I was struck with a memory from when I was about her age, playing with a different band in a similar pub back in Southampton. I'd been dating Ellen for a few months, and that night she'd come to one of my shows like she often did. I'd played my heart out trying to impress her, and when the set was done, she'd come with me back to my flat where she'd showered me with compliments and told me she'd "never felt this way about a man before."

I'd been over the moon, and it was that night I'd first known that I loved her. I'd loved how she made me feel and who she made me be and what I looked like through her eyes.

And that was what felt familiar with Audrey.

I loved how Audrey made me feel. I loved how she made me want to let loose and step out of my comfort zone and be engaged. I loved how she didn't seem to see me as an aging wanker, but as someone interesting. Someone worth spending time with. Someone with something to offer the world.

I loved all of it.

I loved *her.*

I was *in love* with Audrey.

What the bloody fuck was I supposed to do now?

CHAPTER
Nine

I HAD TO AVOID her now, of course. What other option was there for me? It wasn't easy, by any means. By Monday I was in a foul temper, and I'd only been without her for the span of one day.

While everyone at the office was sure to notice my mood, Amy was the only one to mention it. "You're a might prickly today. Want to tell me what bug's crawled up your arse?"

"I've fallen in love with a woman I can't have," I said. There wasn't any reason to keep it secret. I'd always believed in sharing my misery with those closest to me when possible.

"Well, then." Needless to say, she was surprised. "It's not me, is it? Please tell me it's not."

Then we both broke into laughter because the idea was ludicrous. Leave it to Amy to coax out the last bit of cheer from my ornery soul.

"How sure are you that you can't have her?" she asked when we'd settled again.

I sighed and leaned back in my chair. "Very sure." I delivered a brief summary of my relationship with Audrey, skipping over the sexual details out of modesty. "So, you see, she's out to find a life partner, not engage in a torrid affair with a man twice her age."

"Ah. But..." Amy tapped her lip with a single finger. "Is there a specific reason why you couldn't be the life partner she's looking for?"

I chortled, but it ended short when I realized she hadn't meant it as a joke. "That's ridiculous. She's almost twenty years younger than I am. I'm planning my retirement. She's planning half a dozen babies. She's romantic and wide-eyed, and we both know I'm basically Scrooge reincarnated. She wants the fairy tale, and I don't even believe in the customs of matrimony or long-term monogamy. They're outdated and impractical notions."

A deep furrow appeared in Amy's brow. "If you really believe those are flawed traditions, why are you so supportive of her attempt to find a happily ever after? Why not step in, sweep her off her feet, and love her as long as it lasts?"

This was the tough question, the one I'd been grappling with myself for the past thirty-six hours. I was only just now able to confess the answer. "Honestly? Because I'm not sure if they really are terrible customs or if they're just terrible for me."

Amy, my hard-hearted friend, brought her hand to her chest as though she were wounded. "That's very sad," she said sincerely. "Whatever are you supposed to do with your love, then?"

My response was equally sincere. "Suffer in silence. Naturally."

It had been a long time since I'd endured the torment of unrequited affection, however, and the days that followed led to deeper and unbearable despair. Somehow I managed to refuse every one of her calls, replying after with a text saying I was unavailable for the night. Every evening I prayed that she'd get the hint and give up, but she was persistent. Unrelentless.

By the end of the week, my resolve was weakening. I yearned to hear her voice. I ached to know the details of her life. So when she sent me a frantic text Saturday morning, saying once again that she "needed" me, I couldn't help but respond.

DYLAN: What's wrong? What can I do?

AUDREY: I need your help! Can you come over here ASAP?

I wasn't exactly a soft man, but I'd reached my limit of missing her, and I was vulnerable. Against my better judgement, I replied,

DYLAN: I'm on my way.

I began to regret my decision as soon as she opened the front door. She wore only a gray sports bra and low-rise shorts, her hair was thrown up into a mess on top of her head, and all I could think about when I saw her was running my tongue along the rim of her exposed belly button. What did her skin taste like there? Would her voice quiver with excitement like it had when she'd played with herself on camera for me?

It was too late to leave, though, and before I could get my bearings, she'd taken my hand and pulled me inside the flat.

"I really thought I could do it myself, but I'm trying to be better about managing my expectations, and I think I definitely expected too much on this one. Therefore, you must be my hero and rescue me from defeat."

Oh, how I'd missed the sound of her babble. I had more than a little trepidation, however, about being anyone's hero.

She still had my hand in hers with the door shut behind us. "It's this way," she said, tugging me behind her.

While I was distracted by how natural her fingers felt laced through mine, I still managed to assess her living space. It was small and unremarkable. The place had obviously come furnished. They were all dull neutral colors, nothing she would have picked for herself. Her front room doubled as both LOUNGE and dining room. Abstract flower art decorated the walls, but beyond that, it was dreary and drab. Not very Audrey-like at all. The galley kitchen, I noted as we passed, had barely enough room to fit one person, but it did have decent appliances. A multicolored dish towel draped over the tap was the only injection of her personality. Another two steps and we were at the doorway of her bedroom.

She dropped my hand here, which was fortunate since it already felt too intimate to be so close to where she slept, and then swept her arm, introducing me to the space as though she were the hostess on a game show. "Here it is! My project!"

I stepped in cautiously. It was also tiny, barely big enough to fit a double bed, dresser, and nightstand, which was the extent of the furnishings. All three pieces had been gathered in the center of the room and covered with plastic tarps. Painters tape ran along the footboard, and half of one of the dull cream walls was freshly painted in robin's egg blue. More plastic drop cloths were spread over the wood floor, and a paint can of the same robin's egg blue shade sat next to the window with an assortment of brushes at its side.

I had one word for Audrey. "No."

I turned around, ready to walk out of the situation I should never have stepped into. But she grabbed my arm to stop me. "Please!"

"I did not rush over here to help you paint your flat. I thought you'd had an emergency. That you were ill or... or...that someone had hurt you."

"I'll be hurt if you walk out on me."

I scowled in her direction, but she was undeterred. "I *will* be hurt, Dylan! Emotionally hurt, but also physically. I can't reach to the top of the walls, and I don't have a step stool. Anything I try to come up with as a substitution could kill me."

"Hire a painter." I realized after I'd made the suggestion that she likely couldn't afford one. I amended. "I'll hire a painter for you."

"That's silly. It's too small of a space to hire someone. Two people could knock this out in no time." She was so charming, batting her brown eyes, giving me that luscious pout.

My resistance was waning, but for now, it still held. "There's no other poor sap you can rope into laboring on your behalf?"

She peered up at me like I had the power to give her the world. "I'm sure I *could* find someone else, but I don't want to. You've been avoiding me. And I need a man. This just works out, doesn't it?"

I hated that she thought that, true as it was. "I've been busy with a work thing," I lied, unable to give up the pretense.

"Do you have to work on your work thing today? Could you maybe take the day off and spend it with me? I miss you."

I missed her too. Insanely. But while I was happy enough to suffer through my own yearning, I didn't want to ever be the source of her suffering.

I ran a hand through my hair and surveyed the extent of the project again. It really *could* be tackled in one day with the two of us. Painting wasn't so hard. Deciding to do it was.

"It's just these three walls, really," she said, reading my thoughts too well. "I'm leaving the wall above the fireplace the color it is, and I'm doing a design on it with the blue."

I was that fish again, and she was baiting me the way she had when she'd first met me. Falling for the same lure, I had to wonder if I didn't enjoy being caught.

"I'm not wearing clothes fit to paint." I'd already decided to stay, but I wasn't quite done complaining about it.

She looked me up and down. "Do you like your outfit?"

"Should I not?" I couldn't see a thing wrong with what I was wearing.

"It's a fine outfit! I mean, it's a henley and blue jeans. Can't go wrong with the basics."

She was winding me up on purpose. I was sure of it.

"I like this shirt," I said, obstinate.

"Then take it off!"

Grumbling under my breath, I pulled the fleece-lined shirt over my head and tossed it into the hallway. I could feel her eyes on me—ogling, perhaps? I sucked in my stomach and threw my shoulders back, just in case.

She smiled coyly. "If you like your pants, you can take them off too. I won't mind."

I knew then what my gravestone would say—*death by winding*. There was already sexual tension between us before she started plucking at it, pulling it as taut as it could possibly be pulled. Added to that were my newly labeled feelings. I loved her, loved everything about her, and by God, if that didn't make her harder to resist. I wanted her lips, not just because I wanted them, but because I wanted to *love* them. I wanted to love her breasts. I wanted to love her skin and her toes and her cunt, and being trapped with her in a small space while she pranced around in a sports bra wasn't helping the situation.

But I was strong. If I wasn't going to leave like I should, I had to focus on the task.

With a sigh, I headed over to the supplies and selected a large, flat brush, then started on the wall already half done. Audrey poured some of the blue paint into an aluminum tray and chose a brush that seemed more suited for artistry than the task at hand, and went to work over the fireplace.

"Are you even allowed to paint your rental?" I asked after applying several long strokes.

"The landlord said yes, as long as I paint it again when I move out."

The skin at the back of my neck began to tingle. "Does this mean you've been offered the permanent position?

Are you going to stay in London?" Why else would she bother with so much effort if she were only planning to move out in another month or so?

She made a noise that sounded like a vocal shrug. "Nothing's decided yet. But I can't live in this colorless apartment another day. There's no life to it. I can't be this boring."

I looked over at her—a look that was meant to be a glance, but turned into a full stare when I saw what she was doing to the wall she was working on. She'd painted winding strokes coming from the corner and extending across the bare wall. After a few minutes of watching, when she'd begun to outline the shape of a flower, I realized the strokes were stems, and that the abstract art I'd seen earlier had been her originals.

"Those were your pieces in the lounge," I said, wishing I'd studied them longer. "You're quite good."

She laughed and shook her head. "I'm *not*, but thank you for saying so."

"What do you mean? I couldn't even draw a stick figure and make it recognizable. This, on the other hand, is extraordinary."

She stood back to examine her work. "It's all right, I suppose. I spend so much time examining the art of the greats, it's hard to think of my own stuff as something that has value. But I like doing it. And that's pretty valuable regardless of the production quality."

As always, she was wise beyond her years. I had yet to learn the value of a hobby. Everything I did was practical and with reason. I'd only started playing with Thrashheads as a favor to Ian when his bass player had dropped out, and I'd only stayed because I had nothing better to do with my Saturday nights. I'd only learned bass in the first place because my mother had thought that having an instrument on my transcript would look good when applying for uni. What did I ever do that I enjoyed? What did I find value in simply because I liked doing it?

I liked doing this together, actually. Painting, and playing, with Audrey. I could take or leave the actual labor, but being with her, helping her, standing in the same room while she created something that made her smile—*that*, I liked. I liked it a lot.

Enjoying the work made it pass quickly, as well as the small size of the room. By the time two hours had passed, I was applying the second coat of paint on the last wall. Audrey hummed as she painted. Her floral design had taken shape, curling up and around the fireplace like a living vine, and there we were now, at the corner where our walls met, standing entirely too close.

I could feel the heat radiating off her body. I could smell the crisp apple scent of her even through the overbearing fumes of paint. I could sense the tension between us stretching more and more taut. I could barely talk to her, could barely look at her anymore without being in danger of losing my restraint and pulling her into my arms.

Audrey, I surmised, felt none of it. She seemed as cool as a cucumber, even when her shoulder brushed against my arm.

"You've gotten quiet," she said, just when I thought the silence was so thick I'd choke on it. "Are you brooding over something?"

"Only your taste in music. This folk shit is putting me to sleep."

I didn't look at her, but I could feel her body turn in my

direction. "This *folk shit* is quite popular, thank you very much. Excuse me for liking music that's actually musical."

I did turn then. Because, tension or not, I was not about to let her speak ill about the greats of my generation.

"Are you saying that Deep Purple isn't musical? That their guitar riffs aren't among the most recognizable in the world? 'Smoke on the Water' is all I have to say to that." I didn't care if it dated me, I wasn't wrong about rock.

She cocked one hip, and smirked. "I don't know what smoke on the water is. Is that some sort of British saying?"

"You don't—are you saying that you don't know the song 'Smoke on the Water'?" I was practically speechless. I had given her the benefit of the doubt, but this was asking too much. "It's one of the most famous songs of the seventies!"

She raised one shoulder and dropped it again. "I wasn't alive in the seventies. So…"

I drew my lips together in a tight line. "You know it. I promise you know it. We even played it the other night."

"They kind of all sounded the same. I mean, they were really good, but—"

I cut her off with an attempt of the famous guitar line. "Dun, dun, dunnnn. Dundun da dunnn. Dun, dun, dunnn, dundun." She *had* to know it.

She narrowed her eyes and grinned.

"You *do* know it. You're having your fun with me again. Poking at me." I tried, certain my instincts weren't wrong.

"Is that what I'm doing?" She stabbed the air in my direction with her paintbrush. "Poke. Poke."

The next stab was close to me, and I could see exactly

where this was headed. "Don't you dare," I warned.

"Don't dare do what? This?" She waved the brush around threateningly. I leaned back reflexively, dodging her. She laughed and lowered her weapon. Apparently she hadn't meant to paint me with it after all.

Except, as soon as I relaxed, she reached out and swiped across my nose and cheek. I could feel the gooey texture of paint against my skin.

I narrowed my eyes. "You'll pay for that."

"Really? How?"

I wanted to spank her, that's what I wanted to do, but I settled for stroking her across her waistline, that flat stomach that I so wanted to lick. My paintbrush was bigger than hers, so though she'd gone for my face, my hit felt like it had done the most damage.

I bit back a laugh of my own.

Her eyes grew wide. "I can't believe you did that!" She swiped her arm toward me again, striking out toward my chest this time.

Reflexively, I dropped my brush and grabbed her wrist before she could hit her target. The shock of my skin against hers was startling, like the whir of a car engine coming back to life after the battery's been jumped.

I felt resurrected like that in the moment, like I'd been dead and the touch of this woman had brought me back to life. And all I could think about was kissing her. All I could focus on were her lips.

I searched for a sign of permission even as I tugged her toward me.

There wasn't just one, but multiple invitations—the tilt of her chin, her tongue peeking out and dancing across her bottom lip, her eyes big and dilated under the bat of her lashes.

I stopped thinking, stopped holding back, stopped pretending I didn't want her, and pressed my mouth to hers.

CHAPTER
Ten

THE FIRST TIME I kissed Ellen after I knew that I loved her, my world opened up. She'd said she loved me too, and I knew, *I just knew,* that we were headed somewhere together, that we were walking down this path hand in hand, and nothing but bright skies and the future lay before us.

It was a completely different experience kissing Audrey, after I'd accepted the gravity of the feelings I had for her.

I knew the kiss meant nothing, that it would lead nowhere, but it felt like being bathed in radiant light.

Like I was an imprisoned man in a dark prison cell who, for one brief moment, was allowed to step outside into the sunlight. I was completely present for it. Each brush of her lips, each touch of her tongue—I memorized it all, imprinted every second into my brain so that I'd have it forever. I might still have worn shackles with no hope of freedom, but this moment mattered. It was real and divine, and I would cherish every last second of the stolen sunshine until my dying day.

I would've been content with only kissing, with just the shallow lifts and falls of her chest and frantic hands trying to caress and cling.

But Audrey had other ideas in mind, demonstrated by the quick work of her hands at my waist, unbuckling my belt, undoing my trousers, the slip of her hand inside the opening to stroke the outline of my very prominent erection.

"This," she said between kisses. She pulled at the elastic waistband of my boxers and dipped her hand in to touch me directly.

I hissed at the feel of her soft hand against my hot skin.

"I want this," she begged. "Can I have this?"

My cock jumped in her hand at the sweet timbre of her voice asking for pieces of me like she didn't already own the whole. Could she have this? Could she have *me*?

In this moment, yes. She had it all.

It was too erotic, and I was too close too soon. I grabbed her wrists and pushed her back against the wall, in an attempt to gain control.

"You want this?" I rubbed my erection against her belly. "You want my cock so I can fill your pussy like no one else does, don't you?"

She nodded her head vigorously. "Please. Give it to me, please?"

It was like dominoes, how things progressed from there, an event put into action that couldn't be stopped, building momentum in a frenzy of hands and lips and teeth and tongues. I dropped her wrists so I could push up her bra and descend with my mouth upon her sharply pointed nipple. My other hand ventured lower, into her knickers to find the sensitive bud hidden within her folds.

She was wet, so wet I could smell her. So wet that I couldn't resist sliding my hand down her slick crease to plunge inside of her.

"Look at what you have for me." I pulled my finger out and smeared her juices across her bottom lip. "Such a good girl you are, making your pussy all wet and warm for me."

She made a shuddering noise that could only be interpreted as pleasure. While my fingers thrust deeper inside her, I licked across her mouth, a low moan forming at the back of my throat as I rediscovered the wonderful flavor of her desire.

"You taste like a dirty girl. Are you a dirty girl?"

"I'm a dirty girl with *you*. Will you let me come so I can show you how dirty I can be?"

She'd learned well from our lessons of long ago, telling me exactly what she needed.

I leaned back to look at her. She was already tightening around my fingers, but I wanted to watch her face tell me exactly how to make her come, wanted to watch her gaze when she fell apart all over me. Her eyes were hooded and pleading. Her cheeks flushed pink. I bent my finger to rub against her inner wall, and her breath became choppy and unsteady.

I pressed my forehead against hers, letting the bridge of my nose rest against hers. "Show me, then. Show me how dirty you can be and come all over my fingers. If you want my cock, you have to show me how good you're going to treat it. Show me you deserve it."

Her pussy clamped down on my fingers, her body quivering as she let out a strangled cry. Tears spilled from the corners of her eyes. Her mouth froze in a wide O. I pressed my thumb against her clit, coaxing out every last bit of her orgasm.

As soon as it had made its way through her, she was ready for more.

"Need this now. Get it out. Need it." She spoke in short broken sentences while she wrestled with getting my boxers down my thighs. Once my cock was free, she stroked its length with both hands, drawing all the way up with one and following right after with the other. "Let me ride it, Dylan. I want to ride it."

I closed my eyes for a handful of seconds, letting the pleasure of her caress shoot through my body and light up every nerve ending. "Such an impatient girl," I teased.

But I was impatient too. I needed to be buried inside her, and if she kept tugging on my cock like she was, I was going to be finished before we'd truly gotten started.

"Get these off," I ordered, pointing to her shorts. She shoved them along with her knickers down her thighs, stepping out of them and kicking them aside when they reached the floor. She removed her bra when she was done.

Meanwhile, I stripped the rest of the way from my own clothes, then dug my wallet out of my jeans, searching for a condom.

"I don't have a rubber," I said, stepping away from her. If this wasn't going to be able to happen, I needed to be farther away from her. She followed after, throwing her arms around my neck.

"Pill," she said before kissing me. "I'm on the pill."

"I'll pull out," I offered instead, pulling her body flush against mine. I'd known of too many women who'd gotten pregnant while on contraception. My need had reached a desperation point, but I couldn't ruin her life on account of my pleasure.

"Pull out then. Just. Just put it in." She locked one leg around my hips and stood on the toes of her other foot, practically climbing my body to get where she needed me.

Where we both needed me.

Wrapping my hands under the curve of her ass, I lifted her up and backed up against the nearest wall. She threw her other leg around me, and a few short seconds later, I was inside her.

I was inside her, bare, with nothing between her and my cock, and she was heaven.

She was warm and wet and tight—so, so tight. It felt like I was stretching her wider than she'd ever been stretched. Like I was filling her better than she'd ever been filled. Like I was making her into a mold that fit me and only me.

She bucked her hips up, silently spurring me to move.

I became two men in that moment—the one who wanted to take his time and tease and taunt and make it last, another driven by blind lust and the need for satiety. Primal instincts won out, and I thrust into her at an unceasing tempo. I was crazed with my desire. I was the driving beat of a Metallica bassline. I was the prisoner in the yard, chasing the last bits of sunlight, realizing the day was fading into night. I was merciless and mad. I was filled with a love that I couldn't speak of, a love that drummed inside me, begging to be heard.

Audrey took what I gave her, clutching onto my neck as she gasped and moaned and interjected directions on how to fuck her. "Deeper," she'd demand. "Harder. Give me more."

I drilled into her over and over, my thighs slapping audibly against her ass as I gave her the deeper, harder, more she asked for, but still it wasn't enough for either of us. I couldn't get the right angle. Couldn't hit the end of her. Couldn't get deeper, harder, more enough.

Without pulling out of her, I carried her to the plastic-covered bed and dropped her on top. I climbed over her and took up that wicked pace again. It was easier here. I could really thrust in this position, and with my arms no longer holding the weight of her, my hands were free to play with her pussy.

She came right away. "Yes, yes, yessss," she cried, her body clamping so hard on my cock she almost pushed me out. Letting out a grunt, I forced my way back inside, shoving against her wet walls until I was in so far I was sure I was hitting the end of her. I held there, watching as her orgasm rolled over her like a severe thunderstorm, loud and wet and fierce.

I almost came at the sight.

Somehow, miraculously, I remembered in time and pulled out of her. I turned away from her and tugged at my cock a few times.

"No! On me! Come on me." She sat up and lifted her breasts with her hands, giving me a place to aim.

What a fucking turn-on she was—with those pouty, swollen lips and a freshly fucked glow on her cheeks, her legs still spread so I could see her juices gleaming on the folds of her pussy, her perfect, firm tits held up for me to mark.

I came immediately, spurting white ropes of cum across the peaks and valleys of her chest, decorating her with the baseness of my love. Making her dirty and defiled.

Fucking brilliant.

With my orgasm, my adrenaline was shot. We collapsed next to each other on the bed. Sweaty and spent, I closed my eyes and waited for my heart to settle. I could hear her next to me, her erratic breathing settling into a rhythm that matched my own.

"That was...wow," she said. "Just. Really. Wow."

I opened my eyes and looked, not at her, but at the wall in front of me. The wall that showcased her newly painted vines and flowers, as well as an imprint of her backside. I'd pushed her up against the blue wall when I'd finger-fucked her then pressed her to the other wall when I'd had my cock inside her.

"We made a mess of your art," I said, nodding toward the silhouette.

"I like it. I think I'll keep it." The plastic crinkled as she rolled to her side and studied me. "Was this why you were avoiding me? Because you were afraid we'd end up in bed together?"

I turned my head in her direction. There wasn't an easy answer to that question. Even a simple yes or no would be wrong. Neither word completely explained what I'd been avoiding, what I'd been afraid of. What I was *still* afraid of.

"I know I said I didn't want to confuse things. And I think we've both felt the sexual tension building between us. So you stayed away, right? Because you wanted to keep this easy for me. Right?"

Just nod. Let that be the uncomplicated answer.

But all I could do was stare at her, my brow furrowed.

She smiled as though I'd responded. "I appreciate it.

But I think it's a lost cause."

Considering that she was covered in my cum and now had sex art on her wall, I had to agree.

And apologize.

She'd made her wishes known the first night we'd bumped into each other in London, and while she was giving me credit for honoring her request to just be friends, I'd obviously failed at the task. Both because I'd fucked her anyway, but also because I'd developed feelings that were surely unwanted.

But before I could find the words—or the nerve—she scooted into me and nestled her head on my chest.

I put my arm around her, pulling her closer, without even thinking.

"I should have just told you I'd changed my mind." Her voice reverberated against me, causing my skin to buzz.

"What did you change your mind about exactly?" My pulse sped up again, hoping against all hope for something she couldn't be about to say.

"That I only wanted to be friends. Obviously."

She paused. The silence was filled with the hammering of my heart in my ears. Was she saying…? She couldn't want to be *more* than friends, could she?

"I mean, I still want to be friends," she continued. "But I think this is okay, too. Fooling around occasionally. It's kind of perfect, actually. Now I don't have to worry about my libido landing me in bed with a guy I don't actually want to go to bed with."

There was too much to process. Too much needed clarification. I didn't know where to start and ended up just choosing the last thing she'd said, the thing that also happened to be the one that hurt most.

"You still want to date other men, though?" I asked. I needed to be sure.

"Well, yeah. Of course. I still want the happy ending, and I know you aren't after that, but maybe that's what makes this so perfect. You already know that you can do a friends-with-benefits thing and not have it lead to a sticky, complicated mess. I'm the one who has to make sure I don't get attached—and I was worried I couldn't in the beginning, which was why I said that sleeping with you couldn't be an option, and maybe I'm fooling myself thinking I can keep sex and emotions separated, but I want to try."

She leaned up so she could look at my face.

"Do you trust me enough for that? I'm just really attracted to you, and you're really good in bed, and I can't bear the thought of constantly trying to talk myself out of jumping you, but I can't bear the thought of staying away from you either. So if I promise to try really hard, if I promise that any emotions developed are my responsibility and not yours, could we maybe keep doing this on occasion?"

She was anguished with this dilemma. It was written in her face, layered in her tone. It was a complicated predicament, to be fair, and she thought she understood it perfectly. She couldn't have surmised the situation as she knew it any better than she had.

But she was wrong in her breakdown of circumstances. She was wrong in assuming I couldn't have feelings for her too.

If I told her, what would it change? If I were another man, if I were a decade younger, if I weren't someone with enough experience to know that I could never be what she needed, how different would the next part of this conversation go? Would I be man enough to pretend I didn't care?

I wasn't another man, though. I was who I was and that limited my options for response. So, did I tell her I love her and that continuing to sleep with her could be very bad for my heart? Did I tell her and give her the chance to fall for me as well, knowing that as long as we were together, she'd drift farther away from her dream ending of marriage and kids and happiness?

The day's events had changed things, that was undisputable. But I still couldn't stand the idea of ever being the cause of her suffering.

I could only give her what I could, what she asked for, never mind what it did to me. Never mind how much it hurt.

"Don't be silly. I'm not even a little afraid of you falling for me. You have much better taste than that. As for doing *this* on occasion…" I glanced down at the erection that had started to grow again the minute she'd nuzzled up against me. "I think it's obvious I'm interested."

She followed the line of my gaze and a wide smile broke out across her face. "This arrangement is already working out better than I'd hoped."

That smile—that was what made any potential disaster to my heart inconsequential.

I brought my hand behind her head to guide her toward my mouth. Ignoring the tight ache in my chest, I kissed the grin off her lips.

CHAPTER
Eleven

A MY POKED HER head in my office and whisper-shouted across the room. "Is it happening?"

By "it," she meant the biweekly owner's meeting that was conducted over Skype. Often, she'd sit in the room during the videoconference, unbeknownst to my partners, just to provide mocking commentary.

I hit the button on my computer to mute my microphone. "Started about ten minutes ago and everyone's already arguing."

"Oh, tell me!" She hurried in, pulling one of the client chairs from in front of my desk to my side, just out of camera reach.

"Weston says our numbers are higher than they've ever been. Weston's *wife* thinks we should open a new office location in Europe. Sabrina thinks we should open a new office in the States. Donovan is preoccupied with something on his mobile, and Nate is..." I turned my head, examining the window on the screen with his face. It didn't seem like he was in his office, but I couldn't tell where he was instead. He was using a laptop at a kitchen table, maybe, and his focus seemed to be directed at something in his lap.

"I can't figure out what's going on with Nate."

"Got it. Turn it up, will you?"

I increased the computer volume.

"We have demand in Europe *right now*," Elizabeth said from the top right quadrant of my screen. "Clients are coming both to us and Dylan from Germany, which indicates a hole in the market."

"We have demand here too!" Sabrina argued back from the bottom left corner. "We have more than one client that comes from L.A. or Chicago or Atlanta to hire us. New York is farther from all of those places than either Paris or London are to Germany. The need is here." Sabrina nudged her husband. "Tell them, Donovan."

At her prodding, Donovan glanced up toward the camera. "Both Europe and the U.S. present good options for expansion."

Weston blinked as though he'd just caught up with the conversation. "Wait. So we're expanding? We're just deciding on a whim?"

"Honey," Elizabeth said through gritted teeth. "We've been talking about this for months."

"I thought we were just daydreaming, babe. Donovan wasn't involved so I didn't take it seriously."

"Nothing's ever serious until Donovan's involved," Nate said, as though he were part of the conversation, but the way he kept looking down suggested his attention was still devoted to something else.

"Donovan's involved now," Elizabeth said definitively. "The next move is to expand."

"And the expanse should be in the *United States*. Specifically, Los Angeles." Sabrina glared at her husband as if that was the way to coax support.

Donovan hesitated for half a second before looking up from his phone. "We need to see a lot more numbers and projections before deciding on a specific location. I'll hire a demographer to get us some more concrete information."

"He's neither disagreeing nor agreeing with her. That's a talent," Amy whispered next to me.

"Right? He's placating her. It's irritating. He's probably way ahead of us on this, anyway. I'm sure he's already done all the projections and settled on a location that he isn't ready to share with the rest of us yet." Normally I was fine with Donovan's puppeteer methods, but today I was annoyed. With all of them.

I'd tell them, too, if they ever gave me a chance to get a word in edgewise.

"Don't forget there are only five of us." Weston's voice had risen, calling my interest back to the screen. "Who's even going to run a new location? Are we going to start adding more people to this board?"

"Five of us? I count six here," his wife said, annoyed.

"I mean five owners of the company, Lizzie."

"There's seven then because Sabrina and I are now owners by marriage."

Amy and I exchanged an irritated eye roll.

"The point is, *darling*," Weston said, barely keeping an even tone, "that *we're* not going anywhere. We're settled in France. Are you willing to move, D? Or is it going to be you, Nate?"

When neither Donovan nor Nate answered, Sabrina

stepped in. "We don't necessarily need an owner at every office location. Tokyo has been running without one of us for almost a year now."

"That's not exactly an ideal situation," Weston refuted.

"Is Cade ever coming back?" Elizabeth asked. It was the first time our fifth partner had been mentioned in weeks. The meetings where his name had come up previously had unraveled soon after. Cade's leave of absence was a touchy subject, particularly since no one knew details about his departure save for Donovan.

Sabrina once again nudged her husband from his mobile.

"Cade will be back," Donovan said without skipping a beat. "Eventually. When he's ready."

Weston leaned forward. "Are you ever going to tell us what's going on with him, D?"

"No." Donovan returned his gaze to his phone.

"I think there might be a woman involved…" Sabrina started, but if she knew more, she was too loyal to her husband to say more.

"Dylan, you've been quiet," Elizabeth said, sending my brows up in surprise. I was rarely called on in these situations. She had to feel desperate for support. "What are your thoughts?"

"Oh, this ought to be fun," Amy said, rubbing her hands together. "Make it good."

I turned the mic back on, and decided to do just that. "My thought, thank you very much for asking, is that there are entirely too many people involved in these conference calls. When did our team meetings turn into an episode of *The Newlywed Game*? Even you, Nate—am I wrong, or is that Trish's head in your lap?" If he was getting a blow job during our pathetic conference call, so help me God...

Nate's head shot up like a kid caught sleeping in class. "It's the day before Thanksgiving! I'm not even in the office, for Pete's sake. We really should have canceled this today."

"Ah, Thanksgiving. Right," I muttered. "Surely the rest of us should cease our normal business practices because of your bloody U.S. holiday."

"We're planning on celebrating here, actually," Elizabeth said smugly.

Weston's expression softened and he grinned. "We have a lot to be thankful for this year."

"We do," his wife agreed with a sigh.

Jesus fucking Christ.

It took all I had not to slam my fist on my desk. "This is what I'm talking about—could we please keep the googly-eyed, lovey-dovey nonsense out of these meetings? This is a place of business, not a Netflix Christmas special."

Weston, that sad little goof, smirked. "Ah, poor Dylan. I bet it's tough seeing all your friends in relationships that worked out."

"Fuck you very much, King. For your information, I'm more concerned about having to be here when all the romance blows up in your faces." I'd never admit that his analysis of the situation was spot on.

Elizabeth stepped in, as always, to admonish us. "I don't think that was a very nice thing to say."

Her husband was offended. "Him or me?"

"Both of you. I'm not sure Dylan would take that kind of criticism from me, though. Since he's not my husband.

And he's not happy." She tried to bite back a grin and failed.

"I'm right here, you know," I declared, glaring at Amy who was stifling a giggle of her own.

"All right, all right." Donovan stood up and leaned toward the camera, filling up the entire window in his quadrant. "That's enough from everyone. This meeting has officially gone off the rails. We can discuss expanding again at our next meeting in two weeks. Goodbye to all of you."

He and Sabrina disappeared from the screen. Without waiting for the others to bid farewell, I shut down Skype then sunk back in my chair in relief. The madness was over. Praise the lord.

"That went about as well as these things have lately," Amy said after a significant silence had passed. "I should have made popcorn."

"There are too many cooks in the kitchen. That's the problem." And too many emotions. Specifically of the affectionate variety.

Amy moved to perch on the edge of my desk and stared down at me thoughtfully. "I know you don't want to hear this," she said cautiously, "but it seems that your partners have found the right women for them. They're annoying as fuck, and I feel sorry for each and every one of them, but they do all seem to be generally happier since they've settled down."

I narrowed my eyes and snapped. "You're right. I don't want to hear it."

"You do realize that your dim worldview on relationships has been tainted by one relationship."

"I'm a quick learner." I let my smirk fade. "You're also right about the rest. Their relationships are working out, and despite how it appears, I'm very happy for all of them."

"It's still hard to watch. I know. Especially when you're pining after someone you can't have. I definitely know about that." Her eyes glazed like she was remembering something or some*one*, and I wondered for a moment if there was a love story hidden in Amy's past I didn't know about.

But before I could ask, she shook her head and refocused on me. "You haven't been quite that grumpy this week, though, now that I think about it. Did something change between you and Audrey?"

"Not really." I frowned at the incompleteness of my answer. "Yes, something's changed, but also nothing's changed at all."

She nodded. "Ah. You're shagging."

"I didn't say... That's not..." I was flustered, both by her uncanny ability to read me and by the frankness of the observation. "How did you get that out of what I said?"

"We're the same person, Locke." She did a move with two fingers pointing at her eyes and then pointing at me, an eye check, as if to say *I see you*. "I get you."

"I'm glad somebody does." My tone was sarcastic, but in all honesty, I *was* glad that she understood me. Most of the time I felt like a man alone on a raft in open waters. It was an appropriate analogy, in most instances, but it was reassuring to be reminded that others were on the sea alone as well.

"I'm sure Audrey does too, in her own way. And good for you, I might add. Banging is certainly my go-to method of dealing with unwanted emotions."

"You have emotions?" I managed not to crack until she

did. Then I joined her laughter wholeheartedly. It was a nice break to the tension. I could have gone on for a little longer with the joking, in fact, if the phone hadn't interrupted.

I looked at the telephone console. It was my direct line, the line that only three people knew—Ellen, Aaron, and my mother.

"We'll talk later," Amy said, slipping off my desk. She did the *I see you* gesture again as she walked out the door, and I picked up the phone. "This is Dylan."

"Audrey has been in London nearly two months, and still you haven't called me," Donovan Kincaid's voice blasted through the line. Apparently he knew the number as well.

And he wanted to talk about Audrey.

No doubt my outburst during our meeting had led to this confrontation. That hadn't been my intention at all. There were questions I should ask him, yes, but I wasn't ready to confront the answers. I'd been avoiding this discussion with him for that very reason.

I didn't intend to have it with him now, either, if I could help it. "Audrey's in town? Oh, really. That's interesting."

"She already told her sister the two of you are friends. But I understand why you're playing dumb." Fuck, right. Her sister would know that.

It didn't mean I had to confess anything. "I don't have the slightest idea what you're talking about."

"Look, Locke," Donovan's tone said he wasn't in a patient mood. "She's not going to be there forever if you don't take the bull by the horns."

I hesitated. What exactly did he mean by that?

It was probably just a general statement. Or it was a blind stab at trying to wind me up. If Audrey were leaving town, she would have told me. I clung to the same useless tactic. "Again, no idea what you're—"

He cut me off. "Do you need help with what action to take? Is that the problem here? Have you been too long out of the game to get how it's played? I told you this summer, I have ways."

I already had my suspicions about those ways, and since he'd brought it up... "Did you have a hand in her internship at the Gallery?" I asked point-blank.

"I might have dropped her portfolio and application into the email of some important people, but she wouldn't have gotten the job if she wasn't qualified, if that's what you're concerned about."

"Jesus, Donovan..." This was exactly what I didn't want to know. Though I was grateful for every minute that I got to spend in Audrey's presence, interfering in her life was the last thing I wanted to do.

"It's a much better opportunity than the Boston internship, if you ask me," he said, as though that made his intrusion better.

"You're the reason she didn't get that job, too?" The man was clearly out of control.

He bulldozed over my question as though I hadn't asked it. "And frankly, it's a little early in my marriage to have Sabrina's sister living in New York."

"New York?" I didn't try to hide my dismay. "Are you saying there was a job available in New York? Did you interfere with that as well?"

"Another job with limited opportunity. She was much better off in London, and she wouldn't have taken the leap if she didn't have a little push. I did what I could. Don't bother thanking me."

"I'm not planning on it." He'd be lucky if I didn't strangle him the next time I saw him. Audrey would have snatched a New York City offer up in a second. I knew how hard it was for her to be so far away from her sister. Sabrina was her only family.

"You really are a sad sap, you know," Donovan said, changing his strategy. "It's pathetic. You weren't like this when we first met."

"That was over a decade ago. Things have changed. I'm a different person now."

"You are. You're a miserable person, and it's time that you did something about it." He waited a beat before adding, "Or I can do something about it…"

"No," I warned. "Do not do anything else. Do not. Do you hear me? You have done enough, thank you very much."

"I told you not to thank me."

"Donovan," I said, my temper flaring. "Don't interfere."

"I don't think you mean that." Before I could insist that I very much did mean that, he brought up something I hadn't thought of. "If she decides not to stay in London, you're going to want me to make sure she lands somewhere that's good for her."

Well, fuck. He had a point there. I did want the best for her. But did I want it enough to condone Donovan's methods? Now that involved a good hard think. What would be the best thing for me? For Audrey?

"Well, yes," I admitted. "That would be a kind thing

for you to do. For Sabrina's sake." It wasn't me interfering, after all. It was Donovan.

"Speaking of my wife, she said Audrey's been dating a lot."

"Not a lot, really." Though, maybe he knew more about the situation than I did. "Did she say that exactly? That she's dating *a lot*?"

"Obviously it bothers you. I can help you with that."

Dammit, everything he said was a snare, and I'd walked right into this one.

"It doesn't bother me. Why would it bother me?" It was a sorry attempt at backpedaling. Even I knew it.

I let out a frustrated sigh. "I don't know where you got the idea that something is going on between us. I find the girl a breath of fresh air, and we have become friends, but that doesn't mean there is any scheme to try for more. You have to agree we are worlds apart, even if we do happen to live in the same location—temporarily, as you pointed out. I am fond of her, of course. I hope very much that she settles with someone who's good for her."

He paused, and for a moment I thought I'd managed to shut him down. But then he asked, "Are any of these guys that someone? Tell me honestly."

Honestly? That was tricky. I didn't like any of the men she'd told me about so far. None of them were good enough for her, but would anyone ever be? I didn't think it was possible.

What mattered was if she loved them, though. What mattered was if they made her happy. And so far, that wasn't happening.

"No," I answered, digging deep and telling the truth.

"They're not."

"That's where I come in. There are ways to make those relationships—how do I put this? Not work out, so to say. Give me the word, and I'm all over it."

Was that how Donovan thought relationships worked? Disgusting.

On the other hand, it was tempting to consider. While no man would be good enough for her, there were at least men who were better than others. Did I want to be the one to decide who they were?

I did, but not this way.

"I think this is a journey she has to take for herself," I said, finally.

"If that's how you feel, then sure. Let her do that. But call me when you change your mind."

"I'm not going to—" He hung up before I finished my sentence. "I'm not going to change my mind," I said defiantly to the dial tone. Because I meant it.

I wasn't going to change my mind about interfering in Audrey's life.

I wasn't even going to think any more about it as an option.

Probably.

Oh, hell.

CHAPTER
Twelve

I WATCHED AS Audrey scrubbed the remnants of food off her dinner plate. She was careful in her handling of the piece, probably thinking that the china was fine—and it was. Some expensive set acquired during my marriage that I'd ended up with. I'd fought for it in the divorce, as I recalled, for no other reason than that it irritated Ellen to give it up.

The china itself didn't mean anything to me. It usually sat in a cabinet in my lounge, more decorative than functional. I couldn't even remember the last time I'd pulled it out and had only thought of using it today on a whim.

It had been a good inclination, in the end. Audrey couldn't be with her sister for their traditional Saturday post-Thanksgiving Italian dinner, and I'd been eager to do what I could to make the event special for her. The china had been a nice touch. She admired the set more than anyone else ever had.

And I admired *her*. Admired her ease around a kitchen, admired her sass and upbeat energy, admired how she

146 | LAURELIN PAIGE

looked just as beautiful standing behind a sink as she did covered with paint or dressed up to the nines or naked underneath me. Admired how one tiny person could make my flat feel not so overwhelmingly big and empty.

She glanced over and caught me staring. "What?" she asked with a grin.

I shrugged dismissively. "I'm regretting that second helping of dinner."

"I think you had thirds."

"I did. The third helping was marvelous. It's the second helping I regret." I waited for her to laugh before growing serious. "I know I said it already, but the meal was incredible."

"Nonna's lasagna never fails. I'm glad you liked it. It's literally the only dish I know how to make." She finished rinsing off the dish under the tap and handed it to me, sending a pleasant shock through my body when our fingers brushed. "Thank you so much, again."

"For what? Eating delicious food?" I stacked the plate in the drying rack. Normally, I'd leave this task for the housekeeper to do the following morning, but I didn't want Freja asking questions about who I'd dined with. And there were too many dishes to try to say it had just been me.

"Yes, for eating my food. For not leaving me to celebrate today alone. For giving me a magnificent kitchen to cook in." She turned the tap off and dried her hands on a towel before turning toward me and leaning her hip on the counter. "I'm incredibly appreciative."

It felt almost ridiculous to accept her gratitude. It had been a busy week at work for both of us, and though our daily calls had resumed, I hadn't seen her in person since we'd painted her bedroom. I'd missed her and wanted her in my home more than she realized.

I reached around her to dry my own hands on the towel. "I still feel bad that you didn't get a traditional feast on Thursday. If my schedule hadn't been so demanding, I would gladly have taken the day off and celebrated an American Thanksgiving with you."

"Meh. I was working too, and honestly? I couldn't give a flying fig about turkey and cranberry sauce. Today was the day that mattered most to me. You can't have any idea how much it means to me."

"I'm happy to hear that," I said, distracted until we met and locked eyes. I *was* happy to hear it, but it was hard to concentrate on the conversation when her gaze was so intense. And while I adored talking to her always, what I really wanted to do at the moment was turn her around, lift her up on the island behind us, and get under her skirt. I'd been thinking about it since she'd arrived, and had only refrained from jumping her because the dinner was a big deal.

Now, with the table cleared and the dishes done, there wasn't anything to prevent me from acting on the impulse except myself. We hadn't set terms for our relationship, whatever it was now, and I wasn't sure if there were rules. Was I allowed to touch her when I wanted to? Was I allowed to pull her in my arms? Fuck her against the worktop?

It wasn't like me to lack confidence in erotic matters. I refused to doubt myself now. I was going to do it. I was going to devour her. I was going to kiss her lips until they were swollen then go down on her pussy for dessert. Any second now.

In *five*

Four

Three

Audrey broke our gaze and gestured toward the television in the drawing room. "Do you have Amazon Video in here?" She was headed toward the media console before she finished the question, and my opportunity was lost.

I sighed quietly and stared after her. "I do. Is there something you want to watch?" I was content. Well, I could be. Watching my current view, enjoying her backside as she walked away. Maybe content wasn't the right word. She was killing me, literally killing me, with her sultry sway and short pleated skirt. She also wore black knee-high boots and a simple white blouse that made her look even younger than usual. Like a girl in secondary school. Like a girl I didn't have any business lusting after, which only made me want her more.

"It's the next part of the family tradition," she said. She found the remote and stood while she flipped through screens on the telly. "After dinner, we clean up then fall into a food coma on the couch while watching a classic old movie."

"Sounds lovely." The evening was about her, after all. I turned off the kitchen light and followed into the drawing room.

I eyed the sofa. It was too big, not for the room, but for my life. It curved around on one side, easily sitting ten. The most people I could remember having been over at one time was five when my mother, her latest husband, and Aaron had visited at the same time for Christmas. I'd invited Amy over for dinner, hoping my mother wouldn't bother me about my marital status with her at my side. Even then, there hadn't been a time that we'd all sat in front of the telly together. And now, Aaron didn't even come to London to see me very often.

Why had I even bought such a large flat? To show off to Ellen? Certainly I hadn't had ideas of entertaining. It was as though I'd imagined that I could sufficiently fill my life with fine art and furniture and square meterage, but it was all meaningless. I'd never noticed how much so until the vibrancy of Audrey in my space made everything around her pale and dull in comparison.

At the moment I hated how large the sofa was because of how many seating options that gave my guest. I wished for a loveseat instead, something small and cozy where Audrey would have no choice but to cuddle up close.

"What are we watching?" I asked, taking a seat right in front of the screen, the spot where I normally sat when I was alone. The next move was hers.

"One of my favorites. I hope you like it." The show was cued and on pause so I couldn't see what the title was when she spun around and surveyed the seating situation. "Oh good. You saved me a spot." She plopped down next to me, close enough to feel her warmth though not quite so close we were touching.

How did she do that? Deal with the sexual tension between us so easily? It was yet another trait that I admired about her. Another trait that made her irresistible.

She started the show and threw the remote down next to her. The credits started, but I was focused on watching her as she unzipped her boots, dropped them to the floor, and tucked her feet under her bottom.

Jesus. She was wearing plaid knee socks underneath. That basically completed the schoolgirl look. I couldn't look at her if she intended for me to actually get through the film.

I moved my eyes to the screen, a safer place for my attention, just as the title appeared. *When Harry Met Sally.*

"You call this an *old* movie? It's from the eighties." And it was a romantic comedy. She'd neglected to mention that.

She lifted one shoulder and dropped it. "It was made before I was born."

There again with the reminder of our age difference. As if I could forget. "Thank you. Thank you for that," I muttered sardonically.

She giggled, enjoying, as always, a joke at my expense. "Have you seen it?"

"I have not."

"You're going to love it." She side-eyed me as she reconsidered. "Maybe you won't love it, but *I'm* going to love watching it with you, and isn't that what really matters?"

"It seems that it is." And because she then sat back and leaned her head on my shoulder, I didn't have a single reason to argue.

We watched the movie like this for the first ten minutes or so, silent except for her soft chuckle at her favorite lines. The characters, Harry and Sally (who could have guessed), began as two recent college graduates who didn't really know each other but somehow ended up sharing a ride together to New York. They exchanged banter about this and that along the drive, as people do, until Harry stated that it was impossible for men and women to be friends if the man is attracted to the woman—sex always got in the way.

The muscles in my shoulders stiffened. The dialogue could be applied to the situation with me and Audrey. Or, at least, it brought up certain questions about our relationship, and I wasn't sure that I wanted those questions to be asked.

I didn't say anything, hoping that she wouldn't address the elephant if I didn't.

But it wasn't Audrey's style to be demure. "What do you think about that idea?" she asked, casually. "Can men and women be friends?"

"*We're* friends." Maybe she'd leave it at that.

"Buuuuuttt..." She drew the word out, forcing me to give her my attention. "I want to bang you. And I think you want to bang me..."

"Is that a question?"

"You want to bang me. It's not a question. Which pretty much proves Harry's point that men and women can't be friends without sex screwing it up."

"That's where I find his theory objectionable. He assumes that having sex will screw up a friendship-based relationship. I don't find that's true."

"Buuuuuttt..." Again she elongated the word and paused after, as though what she wanted to say next wasn't something I necessarily wanted to hear.

"But what? Let me hear it." I leaned back to stare at her.

She pulled away so she could look at me directly too. "*But* you avoided me for a whole week. That had an impact on our friendship. If we hadn't put sex back on the table, would we be here right now?"

No. Probably not. But not for the reasons she thought.

"Yes, we'd be here," I lied. "Otherwise you're saying that men and women can only be friends if they're sleeping together. In which case, I really need to reevaluate all my female friendships." It was a joke, but if it weren't, there was really only Amy on that list, and I *had s*lept with her in the past. Was she right?

"Except, then someone might develop feelings."

The back of my neck suddenly felt sweaty, and my throat felt tight. I swallowed. "People might develop feelings even without sex."

"True. It's just easier to encourage feelings when sex is involved because of the intimacy level. And what happens when one of the partners decides to end the sexual part of the relationship? Is it possible to go back to being just friends?"

The question felt important, as though it were a test, as though my answer said something significant about us. Amy and I had managed to maintain our friendship with or without benefits, but I was wary about saying yes to Audrey because I wasn't entirely certain that I could ever go back to being just friends with her.

But that wasn't because of sex. That was because I had already developed feelings for her. Not that she needed to know that. In fact, she really *didn't* need to know it.

I hesitated too long with an answer. "You don't think it's possible, do you?" she asked. "So when I eventually find a guy that I want to be with, are you and I just done?"

"No. Of course not." It was another lie.

"Buuuuutttt…"

I ran a hand through my hair. "We won't be *just done*. But a lot changes when you get involved with someone romantically. I'm sure you know that. Often, other relationships are not what they were. They take a backseat, whether there's a sexual history or not. So while I can promise that sex is not the glue holding our friendship together, I can't promise that we'll always be as close as we are now." It was more of a monologue than she'd wanted, perhaps, but it was honest, though maybe it wasn't the complete truth.

Because the complete truth was hard to say to some-one like Audrey. The complete truth was that nothing lasts forever. Not even good things. *Especially* not good things.

Audrey settled back down next to my shoulder. "You're a real Debbie Downer sometimes, Dylan. You know that?"

"I do, in fact. It's an actual bullet point on my resume."

She pretended not to chuckle. "Do you need me to rewind?"

"No, I think I have the gist of what's going on."

The movie got better after that, or at least, less uncomfortable to watch. The writing was decent. The characters were well drawn, particularly the side characters. Some of the dialogue felt contrived, but it was enjoyable for the most part. I kept my comments to myself when it wasn't.

Until the public orgasm scene.

It was a famous bit. I'd seen clips of it before, but never in context. Harry was convinced that all the women who came into his bedroom through a revolving door, enjoyed themselves. In response, Sally faked an orgasm—in public—to prove that there was no way he could possibly tell.

"Oh, please," I mumbled.

Audrey sat up and narrowed her eyes in my direction. "You have to expand on that comment. You can't possibly think women don't fake orgasms."

"I'm sure they fake them all the time, though I'm not entirely sure what the benefit is from that. If men think the woman they're with is satisfied, they're not going to put forth more effort." It was common sense. "But that's not what I find eye-rolling."

"They fake it sometimes because it's just easier. Like, it's not happening, and some men are so stubborn, they prolong the whole thing in an attempt to *make* it happen, and that's miserable for everyone."

"You sound like you speak from experience." If Audrey had similarly faked orgasms with the men she'd been with before me, no wonder there had been a problem in the bedroom.

"I do speak from experience. Not with you." Her cheeks pinked ever so slightly.

"Of course not with me."

And now I was thinking about making her orgasm. The sly smile on her lips suggested she was thinking the same thing.

But then her grin disappeared. "But tell me what you find eye-rolling."

I changed my seating position, adjusting myself discreetly, and sighed. It had been me who'd triggered the conversation. I had to back it up, no matter how smug I came across in doing so.

"While it's true that men can't always know if a woman is having an orgasm or not, there are a lot of tells that are easy to spot if one is simply paying attention. Nonvocal tells. Changes in breathing. Body quivering. Flexing of toes. Contractions of the...of the inner walls of..." If I said the word, if I mentioned her pussy, I was going to have to be inside it.

"You get what I'm saying."

Her blush deepened, as though she could read the thoughts in my mind. She cocked her head to the side.

"And you don't think a woman can fake all those things, sometimes?"

"She can, but it's my experience that most women don't even know what her tells are. It's difficult to fake something you don't know to fake."

"But if it's a one-night thing, the man doesn't know what her tells are, either."

"This is true. But if it's only one night you're spending together, why would the man even care?" It was terrible to say, but men could be terrible where sex was concerned. Men could be terrible, full stop.

"Harsh!" Audrey twisted her lips, pondering. "Are you saying you didn't care if I orgasmed that first time when you fingered me against the front door at your apartment?"

"It was different with you." My cock twitched in my trousers, remembering.

"Of course it was different with me." She repeated my words from a minute before.

"It was, though. You had specifically come to me with a request to have good sex. It didn't behoove either of us if I didn't put my best foot forward."

"Your best *finger* forward, you mean. Three of them, to be precise."

"I'm very flattered that you remember so well." Very flattered and very hard.

"It wouldn't have *behooved* me to forget." Her grin was so fucking sexy. I wanted to finger-fuck it off her face. With three fingers. "And I don't believe that you would ever not care about giving a woman an orgasm. You're very considerate like that. A true gentleman."

"And you're cheeky."

She moved to her knees, and faced me, the movie apparently forgotten. "What are my tells? Are they obvious?"

"You stop breathing." It was incredibly erotic. Her muscles would stiffen, her toes curl, and her quick breaths would all of a sudden stop, like she was bracing for the pleasure to hit. Then, when it finally did, she'd moan her release, her body stuttering as it rolled through her.

"Hmm. I guess I do." She was pensive suddenly, her eyes downcast. "I guess that's an easy thing to tell a new lover. 'Look for my breathing to stop, and then you know you've hit the spot.'"

My chest felt tight, like my insides were shrinking. Here I was thinking we were having a fun talk about us and what she was really thinking about was her future. About the guy she'd be with next, whoever he was.

But that was always the point of us, from the very beginning. Wasn't it?

I forced a weak smile. "There you go."

Her expression softened. "I don't have a new lover," she said quietly. "In case you were wondering. Besides you. I'd tell you if I did."

"Okay."

"I thought you should know that."

It was as though she knew what she'd said hurt me, as though she were trying to make it better. Which, of course, she wasn't. She couldn't know what was going on inside me. She was merely being considerate to her sexual partner. It was practical.

"I also have no other lover," I said, returning the consideration. "In case you were wondering."

"We'd stop this between us if anyone else came into

the picture, right? Can we agree on that? Especially if we aren't going to use condoms. And we don't need to use condoms. I'm really good about the pill."

"We can agree on that." I didn't want to talk anymore about other lovers. I didn't want to think about her needing to be on birth control because of other men. I hoped this pact put an end to the subject.

Unfortunately, it only got worse. "I do have a third date with someone this week."

Discovering Ellen's affairs had felt like a dagger in my gut, and yet still these simple words from Audrey felt ten times worse. She'd been dating—I'd *known* she'd been dating—but this was the first time anything had ventured on being serious.

I played nonchalant. "Oh? A third date?"

I didn't want to hear more. I had to know everything at the same time.

"The first two dates were promising." She pushed a stray hair behind her ear and shifted to sit on her hip. "He's a decent enough guy. Catholic. Wants a big family. He's an architect, so that's a stable career. And he gets my artsy side. He has a really cute little Yorkshire terrier that he brought to our first date in the park. I'd marry him just to have that puppy. He seems really romantic, too. Says a lot of flowery things. Loves poetry. His name is Marco. He's the brother of one of the married guys I work with. He's Italian! Nonna would be over the moon if she were still alive."

Every word she said was bittersweet. Sweet because he sounded great. Bitter because I wanted to stab this Marco guy with a knife between the eyes. Several times. Twenty ought to do it. And I'd never been one for violence.

But I could see the bigger picture through the red. His qualities were perfect—perfect for Audrey, anyway. And wasn't that exactly what I wanted for her? A man who would give her everything she wanted, everything she needed. A man who loved her as much as she deserved to be loved. A man who could make her happy. If this was that guy, then I wanted it to work out for her.

Just, I wasn't ready to let her go.

"I'm not planning on sleeping with him," she said reassuringly. "So don't worry about that. Not yet anyway. I haven't even kissed him. So there's no reason for this to end." She gestured between the two of us.

"Okay."

So she wasn't done with us yet either, then. Not yet, and I meant to take advantage of that.

I turned again to the screen, not really watching it, but planning my move.

"That was an invitation, by the way," Audrey said at my side, always a step ahead of me.

I pushed her back on the couch and crawled over her, pinning her hands over her head. "Was it now? I'm allowed to stop watching this sappy chick flick then, but only if I instead turn my focus to draining every last drop of cum from your pussy?" My cock had softened during her talk of other lovers, but now it was back to full mast.

I bucked against her so she'd know.

"It's an invitation, not an obligation!" she giggled, and I kissed her. Kissed her hard.

"Your pussy is never an obligation," I said when I came up for air. "You're very naughty for even thinking it could be."

"I *am* naughty. I deserve to be punished, don't I? Are you going to spank me, Daddy?"

God, she was perfect. She'd probably meant to dress like a schoolgirl. She knew it would drive me mad, and it did.

She'd pay for that.

"Daddy has another punishment in mind, and you'll take it like a good girl, won't you?"

She squeaked out a *yes* that made me growl.

"Right answer. Take off your knickers." I slapped the side of her thigh then pushed off her and made quick work of unfastening my trousers and sliding my boxers down my thighs. I was too impatient to take them off any farther, and I had what I needed available and ready for her.

And she was ready for me, her knickers now discarded on the floor.

I sat back where I'd been sitting before and reached for her, intent on pulling her onto my cock, which was throbbing and red for want of her. But then I noticed her dazed expression. She wet her lips with her tongue and I followed her gaze to the swollen staff between my legs.

She wanted it in her mouth. It was all over her face. Those were the kinds of tells I was talking about.

I stroked my fist up and down my length. "You think you can suck me good, Audrey? You think you can take all of me and make it good?"

She blinked her lashes exaggeratedly. "I don't know if I can," she said, feigning innocence that she didn't truly possess. "It's so big. Would you let me try?"

A drop of cum leaked from my tip, I was so turned on.

"You may try."

Her eyes never left mine as she knelt on the sofa and bent over me. She had to turn her head to maintain the contact as she took my crown into her mouth, and God, it was perfect. So perfect. Her mouth was hot and wet and heaven. She wrapped her small hand around the base and eased the length of me back toward the inside of her cheek. My head rubbed against the inner wall of her mouth sending electric sparks of bliss down my spine. I let out a low hiss of pleasure.

Then she changed her angle, and this time when she sucked me back, she took me in deep. She hollowed out her cheeks, increasing the friction along my shaft and making me shudder.

She was so bloody sexy. So goddamned provocative. I was in near mindless ecstasy, but I needed to touch her. I needed to taste her.

I reached my hand around her backside and underneath her skirt. I smacked her once, and she yelped. The sound vibrated against my cock, sending another euphoric spasm through my body. I gritted my teeth and focused on not coming. She'd take my cum, she'd swallow all of it, I was sure, but I wanted to be wrapped in her pussy when I released. At the rate this was going, I'd need to make sure that happened soon.

I needed to get her ready.

My hand trailed along her slit until they found her hole. She was wet. Dripping wet. So wet that three fingers slid in easily.

"You're such a naughty girl, aren't you? Getting so aroused from sucking my cock. You love it, don't you? Tell me how much you love it."

She dragged her lips slowly up my erection. My crown

fell out of her mouth with a loud pop. "I love it so much. I love how big you are. You make me so wet."

I had to have her mouth, that dirty mouth. Had to taste it and inhabit it. Had to be inside her with my tongue the way I needed to be inside her with my cock.

I clamped my palm behind her neck and drew her close. She came to me like a magnet, like we were meant to clash together. Like we couldn't be apart.

We kissed fiercely, our mouths twisting and slipping against each other while she climbed over me, her legs straddling my thighs. With one hand still braced behind her head, I used the other to guide myself inside her slick cunt. She trembled as she slid down my length, and I swallowed her accompanying cry.

I know, I told her with my kiss.

I know how good it feels. You make me feel that good too.

She rode me then, with vigor, her hips bouncing up and down over my cock like it was her vocation. I broke away from her mouth to watch her and nearly fell apart. She was a kinky little wretch, squeezing at her pert breasts through her blouse, her orange pleated skirt hitched high on her thighs. She looked like a goddamn Britney Spears video. A vixen of a schoolgirl, writhing on the plumpness of my cock.

"Don't pull out," she said, her breathing rapid. "I want you to fill me up."

I was going to burst any second, she was so fucking hot, but I needed her to go with me. My thumb reached under her skirt and found the button of nerves hidden under the hood of skin. It only took a handful of swipes before her muscles were tensing and her breathing turned rapid.

Just as she stopped breathing all together, I gripped my hands on her thighs and ploughed up into her, fast and hard and insistent until we we were both there together, gasping and shattering apart as one.

I kissed her leisurely for a long time after, my cock half soft but still planted inside her. When she eventually crawled off of me, I groaned at the loss of her heat.

"My legs are asleep," she said, as though I deserved an explanation. As though there couldn't be any other reason why she'd want to get off my cock.

I liked believing that, anyway.

She curled up next to me, laying her head on my chest. I didn't want to move, didn't want to let her go, so I didn't tuck myself away. I just held her, placing soft kisses along her apple-scented hair. We didn't talk. We didn't say anything at all.

The movie had continued during our activity and was now near the end. I found myself caught up in its ending when Harry finally realizes Sally is the woman meant for him and runs to her, bursting into the party she's at on New Year's Eve so he can win her heart with a speech that could only have been written by a woman. It was so sappy and moving.

It wasn't a spoiler of an ending, even having missed a good portion of it. It was a rom-com. That was how all of these things ended, a blissful, happy myth. It was a lie, but instead of being annoyed like I usually was by it, I found I felt sad.

"I want that," Audrey said softly.

I wanted that too. Everyone did. That was what made it so easy to sell.

"It doesn't have to be a speech," she continued when

I didn't say anything. "It doesn't have to be a party. It doesn't have to be any of that specifically. I just want the guy. I just feel like it's never going to happen some days."

She sounded as melancholy as I felt, and I hated that. It was one thing for me to be a scrooge, but not her. Not yet. She deserved years of living the fable before she discovered that endings were never happy. Hell, maybe she could even go through a separation without being broken. If I hadn't been so antagonistic with my ex-wife, maybe... but it didn't bear thinking about.

I kissed her on the top of her hair and summoned up the advice she needed, the advice I would have wanted when I was where she was in life, innocent and foolish and eager.

"That's a lot of pressure you're putting on the universe, to have things happen on *your* timeline, in *your* way. It doesn't give fate a chance to work the perfect ending you're waiting for. I think this is a case for that old adage—if you love something, set it free. If you believe that fate will bring you the guy you belong with, then stop trying to force it. Stop trying to predict it. Stop trying to rush it along. Let the idea of falling in love go. It will come back to you when the time is right."

She was quiet for several beats. Since she wasn't facing me, I couldn't see her eyes, but she made a noise that sounded like a sniffle, and I wondered if she was trying not to cry.

If she was, she managed to hold it in because her voice was clear when she spoke. "That's very optimistic of you, Dylan. I'm impressed."

I chuckled. "I fail to see how having no expectations is optimistic."

She shifted so she could see me. "No expectations? Do

you really not expect anything from your future? I understand letting go, but giving up?"

Perhaps she felt my pep talk to her deserved one in return, but I was long past giving up. Her words of hope and encouragement were worthless, delivered in vain.

"Of course I have expectations," I said, kissing her on the nose. "I expect another round riding your pussy in about ten minutes."

Her eyes grew dark and hooded. "Why ten minutes?"

"Because first I'm ready for dessert." I pushed her onto her back and went down. She tasted like me and her together, and my dick hardened again, but I ignored my need and devoted myself to pleasing her. Only her. I ate her like I was a starving man. Like I was a man who still had a chance of being saved. Like I was a man who wasn't already dead inside.

CHAPTER
Thirteen

A S AUDREY'S THIRD date with Marco approached, I found myself more and more restless. More and more *jealous,* to be precise. It was easier to push aside when I was with her, when she was in my arms and my cock was lodged firmly inside her, but when we were apart, my mind latched onto thoughts of her with him, thoughts of him kissing her and seducing her. I had a solid picture of him in my head—dark unruly hair, thick biceps, a charming smile that persuaded unsuspecting young women like Audrey to hand over their knickers with a gift-wrapped bow.

Wanker.

It was ridiculous how much I thought about it. She'd been out on other dates, and I hadn't been so bothered. Mostly because my truth was that I was the man who got to talk to her before she left for her dinner or her play or her game of bowling, and I was the man who talked to her when she came home. Others had her for a few hours, but I was in her bed. And because of that, it had been hard to take her dating seriously.

But she had never had a third date.

She'd never even had a second date, and this new development haunted me. Marco became an obsession. Google became my enabler. I typed in combinations of what I knew—his name, his occupation, his religious denomination. I felt crazed as I searched for him. This wasn't me. Why was I acting like a stalker?

But I couldn't help myself. I was out of control.

Even as I told myself to stop, I couldn't. It wasn't like me, but then, nothing about Audrey was like anything I'd ever experienced.

I was a wanker, too.

When Google led to nothing, I had a chance to stop myself. I told myself to stop being a loon and focus on my work like a normal, rational person. I told myself to shut my browser and step away.

Then, somehow, like a mad man, I found myself on the Gallery website studying the staff listings. I paired the surname of every male on the roster with Marco's name, typing them into Google one at a time until I hit a match. Marco Ceresola. He was on Instagram.

Jesus, fuck, I muttered to myself. He was even worse than I imagined. His skin was flawless, his eyes large and piercing. Apparently a six-pack wasn't good enough for him. He had to go and get an eight-pack, which I only knew because of the countless images he'd posted of himself bare-chested. And that damn Yorkie was pussy-bait. There were more pictures of that ball of fur than of its owner. Adorable photos that made even the hardest of hearts melt. I was half convinced *I'd* drop trou for that puppy, and I neither cared for dogs nor men.

I couldn't go on like this.

I was barely sleeping. I was irritated and jittery from copious amounts of Earl Grey. I was out of my mind with envy. Yes, yes, I wanted the best for Audrey, and if the outside image was all there was to know about a person, then Marco Ceresola was absolute perfection, but in my experience, the story projected to the public was rarely the real story. Or at least, not the *whole* story.

Without any real proof, my gut said this guy was bad news. My head knew I was overreacting, but I didn't care. I had to do something about it before she made a mistake and fell in love. Before she got her heart crushed. Before I went insane.

Thursday afternoon, one day before the big date, I settled on exactly what that something was—I had to ring Donovan. He'd take care of my dilemma. He'd offered often enough, but I hadn't been desperate to take him up on it. Marco, though... Marco made me desperate.

I shut my office door for privacy and pulled out my mobile. I flipped through my contacts and found Donovan's information.

My thumb hovered over the call button as I hesitated. Once Donovan was involved, there was no turning back. He wasn't the kind of man who tolerated flakiness. I considered what I wanted my friend to do, exactly. Set a tail on Audrey to be there in case she got in trouble? Get rid of this boyfriend altogether? Get rid of all her boyfriends?

That was the rub, wasn't it? As soon as I got involved once, it made the line of interference immovable. I was always going to be That Guy. Either I had to let Audrey live her own life and make her own mistakes, or I'd be in this endless pursuit of trying to make her life perfect for her.

And I already knew there was no such thing as a happy ending. So what was I expecting from that course of action?

I couldn't do it, couldn't intrude. But I couldn't just wait around and obsess while she lived her life, either. A distraction was necessary.

I put my mobile down and returned to the Gallery's staff webpage. A few clicks and I had the number I was looking for. I picked up my phone again and made the call.

Midway through my dinner the next night, I realized I'd made a big mistake.

As painful as it was to sit at home while she went on a date with Marco, going on a date of my own was even more miserable. Especially going on a date with Jana Spruce.

I'd thought it had been a rather practical idea when I'd had it. If Audrey was going to be dating, I should too. Not because I was looking for the same thing that she was—I wasn't. But it seemed like a good way to occupy my mind while she was off trying to find her happily ever after. If I only went out on one date, two at the most with the same woman, no one could become attached. I wouldn't bed them. I might even gain something from it—a nice meal, good company and conversation. The plan sounded perfect.

It was only a coincidence that I chose Audrey's boss to be my first date. Since I hadn't been looking for a woman to ask out, my choices had been limited, and Jana Spruce had hit on me the night I'd met her at the fundraiser anyway. It had only barely crossed my mind that Jana might tell her subordinate about our evening out. I hadn't fancied that Audrey would find herself in the same jealous torment that I was in.

Well, I hadn't *overly* fancied it anyway.

The evening with Jana had started well enough. The restaurant had been my choice, so the food was excellent. The service was above satisfactory. Jana was punctual and looked nice. She was smart and interesting and attractive and was a superb storyteller. She was a divorcee with two kids who were near Aaron's age, and that gave us a lot to talk about. I didn't normally date women who had parenting in common with me, and it was, it turned out, a pleasant change. She was also very funny, though I failed to laugh at most of her jokes. That had nothing to do with her—it was a *me* problem. I saw the humor, saw the wit in her jokes, but I saw Marco and Audrey far more vividly. Even in the midst of engaging conversation, Audrey's date was foremost in my mind.

Which was why the entire night was a disaster. I hadn't distracted myself from anything at all. I'd only proven that I was very capable of multitasking my agony.

And agony was much better performed with no distractions for optimal wallowing.

As soon as Jana excused herself to use the loo, I reached for my phone in hopes of a message from Audrey. I'd been itching to look since dinner began. Though Audrey usually didn't contact me during her dates, I hoped that this time was different. Hoped that Marco had bailed on her or that she'd bailed on him or that she was bored or dismayed or *something. Anything.*

There was nothing. Not a single notification from anyone. My stomach sank at the implications. She didn't need me. She didn't want me. She was having a nice night. And it didn't involve me.

170 | LAURELIN PAIGE

I pocketed my phone, but pulled it out twice more to look again before Jana returned. The last time I even rebooted it, just in case there was an issue with my mobile or the service connection.

"Is there something you need to attend to?" Jana asked when she returned and found me staring at my screen.

"No. Sorry. Just checking my messages." With a sag of my shoulders, I put my phone away, but even with it back in my jacket pocket, I could feel it burning against my chest, ceaselessly nagging for my attention.

Jana was quiet as she took a swallow of the brandied latte she'd ordered in lieu of dessert. I'd hoped she would have skipped the course all together so I could get back to my pining. I'm not sure I didn't sigh audibly when she asked to see the coffee menu. It would be over soon enough. Another ten minutes, probably, at most. I could be patient.

"Can I ask you something?" Jana asked studying me.

I nodded, afraid if I actually spoke that she'd hear the irritation in my tone.

"Why am I here?"

"I beg your pardon?"

She shook her head dismissively. "A better question is why are *you* here? I'm sure you realize that I fancied you that night we met, and I was excited when you reached out. I didn't think for a minute that you were interested in anything serious. A smart, sexy man like you would have a woman if he wanted one. I assumed when you called that you were looking for the same thing that I am—companionship. I'm certainly not keen on marrying again or even getting involved in a relationship, but I do enjoy a good lay as much as the next woman. If that's why you're here, then all we need to work out is your place or mine.

"However, you've seemed distracted all evening. So you tell me—am I reading you wrong? Why are you here?"

My brow furrowed. I'd already realized that I was here for all the wrong reasons, but now I felt like a total heel as well. It hadn't occurred to me she'd recognize my angst. I *wasn't* interested in pursuing a relationship, but I did know that people came to a date with something to offer. I'd figured a paid meal and engaging company was enough—and it likely would have been, had I actually been engaging.

But that wasn't the reason I hesitated in my response.

I hesitated because it finally hit me how fucked up I was over Audrey. A handful of months before, I wasn't actively dating, but I would have welcomed a no-strings attached physical relationship with an attractive woman like Jana. I would have gladly taken her home and put out.

I still could. I could invite her to my flat and fuck her on the couch and against the kitchen sink and over the dining table and everywhere else that Audrey had been and touched. Maybe that would be the distraction I needed. Maybe if I fucked someone else, I'd remember that there were other cunts in the universe, that there were other attractive women worthy of spending physical time with.

But I didn't want to take Jana home.

I didn't want to use another woman to fuck away thoughts of Audrey. It wouldn't be fair to either of them. And it was new to me to have such a thought. Fair wasn't a concept I typically considered.

"I'm not sure why I'm here," I said finally. "I fear I've been a terrible waste of your time. I apologize sincerely, and please, rest assured that as cliché as it sounds, it's not you. It's most definitely me."

"Please," she teased. "I know it's not me. I'm a hell of a catch." She was a confident woman, and I usually found that a turn-on. What a waste of a good evening, for both of us.

"You *are* a catch. At another time in my life, maybe…" I trailed away because it wasn't polite to offer hopes I couldn't back up.

Jana tilted her head. "What *are* you looking for at this time in your life? If you don't mind me asking. I'm not trying to change your mind, I'm simply curious."

"Well, that's a good question." I ran my hand along my trouser leg under the table as I decided how to answer. "I suppose I'm like you, looking for some companionship now and then. Nothing permanent. No committed relationships for me anymore. Been there, done that."

"Your marriage ended as badly as mine did, did it?"

"It did." *Bad* was an understatement. *Permanently scarring* was a better term. *Completely destructive* was another. "Yes, I know one bad experience doesn't mean they're all going to be terrible, but it was *really* terrible. And painful. And a hassle, in the end, arguing over custody and record albums that neither of us are ever going to listen to again. It killed something in me, I think. I was an awful person through it all and a horrible father. I was mean and distracted and sad. So very sad. I had to go numb inside in order to survive it."

I was *still* numb. Or I had been until Audrey.

"If I did ever fall in love again," I said, omitting the part that I was already in love with someone we both knew, "I'm afraid I'd never be able to fully commit, even if I wanted to. I'd constantly be bracing for the other shoe to drop. I'd be guarding myself, waiting for the end to come.

I don't believe that I'd ever be able to give my whole heart, and I know enough about successful relationships to know that's one of the most important ingredients."

I stayed caught in the thought for a moment when I was done talking, letting the things I'd said sink in. I'd been more truthful than I'd intended to be. It was the most honest I'd been with another person about the subject. It was the most honest I'd ever been with *myself.*

Jana put her mug down and scooted it away. "You know. After you came to the fundraiser with Audrey and gave that generous donation that secured a position for her, I thought the two of you might be involved."

"No, no, no." I realized I'd been too eager with my denial, both to Jana and to myself. And as long as we were being truthful… "It's one-sided, anyway. She's a very special young lady, as you surely know, and I am tremendously fond of her. I wouldn't ever put that upon her because she's looking for the whole romantic picture—the groom and the picket fence and the children—and that's obviously not something I'm able to offer. But I do care for her, greatly. I wish her to receive every opportunity available, and I suppose I crossed a line in donating that money. I simply wanted her to be able to stay here if she liked, and I let my affection for her get the better of me."

"I understand. She is very special." *And too young for you.* She didn't say it, but she had to be thinking it. "Has she said that she wants to stay here?"

I frowned. "No, she hasn't." We hadn't actually talked about it. I'd simply assumed. "Has she said something to you?"

"No. But she hasn't accepted the job either. And if she doesn't, I wondered if you expected the money to be returned or if you would allow us to allocate it elsewhere."

174 | LAURELIN PAIGE

"Oh. I didn't realize that." It felt like an anvil was suddenly pressing against my chest. It was hard enough getting used to the idea of sharing Audrey with other men. It was much harder to accept if I didn't get to have any part of her at all.

I didn't want to accept it. I wanted her here. I wanted to tell Jana that she had to make the offer more attractive. I'd double the donation. Whatever it took.

But that was interfering too, wasn't it? When I'd decided that I wasn't going to do that.

I let out a heavy sigh. "Of course you can use the money how you please. I only wanted to give her the opportunity. Is there a deadline for her acceptance?"

"The show she was brought on to help with opens tomorrow, so her internship is winding down. I told her I needed to know by December tenth."

It was the last day of November. That gave me ten days. Ten days to hope she'd decide to stay. Maybe she'd stay for Marco. My stomach twisted at the thought, and I bit my tongue so hard I tasted blood.

But at least she'd still be here, I told myself. Surely that was worth the anguish.

It was. It had to be.

My dinner date was over, and I was even more miserable than I'd been when it had begun. I paid the bill, and we walked outside together where I hailed Jana a cab.

"You sure you don't want to come over? I'm a great nightcap."

I was tempted this time more than I had been before. My interest level hadn't changed, but I was sure it would be good for me. I needed to fuck away my Audrey attachment, even if I didn't *want* to.

But that didn't feel fair to anyone. I wasn't even sure I could get it up.

I thanked her again and sent her away before hailing another cab for myself. I checked my phone as soon as I was on the road and found nothing had changed since the last time I'd checked. I stared out the window at the Christmas lights and composed a hundred different messages to Audrey that I never planned to send.

How did your date go?

Are you happy with him?

Will you stay in London for him?

Will you stay?

It turned out I didn't have to send a single text to get at least some of my answers. Because as soon as I walked through the lobby of my building on the way to the lift, I spotted her sitting on the stairs. Her shoulders were slumped and the corners of her mouth were bent into a frown.

"My phone died," she said, her voice thick. "I didn't have anywhere else to go so I just waited for you here."

She was obviously upset. I immediately tensed, ready to take action. "Did the asshole hurt you?"

"No. I think I might have hurt *him*."

"Physically?"

She shook her head. "He wanted more. But he's not The Guy, so I can't give him more. I can't force it."

I didn't know how it was possible to be elated and hurt for her at the same time, but I very much was both.

"I'm taking your advice, Dylan. Letting go of the idea

of love. Here's to hoping it comes back."

My feelings for her bubbled abruptly inside my chest, rising through my throat, pressing to escape in the form of words. *I'm here. I love you.*

But it wasn't the kind of love she wanted, and even if it was, it wasn't the love she deserved.

I held out my hand and offered her the only thing I could give instead. "Want to go upstairs and get fucked for being such a good little girl, making such a grown-up decision?"

She took my hand. "Yes. Yes, I do."

CHAPTER
Fourteen

"FANTASTIC SHOW, AUDREY," I said as we walked out of The National Gallery. "Simply splendid. Brava." It was opening day of the Christmas exhibition she'd been working on, and she'd just finished taking me through the display. It had truly been awe-inspiring to see her in her environment. I couldn't stop grinning.

Her cheeks flushed the way they did when I was balls deep inside her. "I don't really deserve any credit for it. It wasn't *my* show. Mostly I pulled things from the archive room and got people coffee."

I looked at her curiously. False modesty wasn't like Audrey. Either she truly hadn't done much or she believed that she hadn't. "Nonsense," I said sincerely. "You knew each and every piece inside and out. Your commentary was the highlight of the exhibit. You can't have that much knowledge about the project if you weren't deeply involved."

She hesitated, as though she wanted to accept my

words, but wasn't so sure. "No, honestly. I'm just an intern. Anyone could have done what I did."

"But not anyone did. You did, and they hired you for a reason." And they'd offered her another position as well. Was that the real reason she hadn't accepted? Because she didn't feel confident?

She considered. "I suppose that's true. And I really did love the work. And the people at the museum. It's definitely been a dream job, even though it was mostly grunt-work."

Then take the offer, I thought. Stay and climb the ranks.

I didn't say it though. She didn't know that I knew she hadn't accepted, and while I could just ask her what she was doing next, I was too afraid of the answer.

There were still ten days until she had to give her decision to Jana. Nine and a half now. I planned on making them the best days possible, hoping she'd be happy enough to want to stay.

"You'll let me take you to dinner now to celebrate, won't you?" My mind was already working through the restaurants I knew in the area that didn't need a reservation. We'd want to go someplace close or else get a cab. It hadn't started snowing yet, but the forecast had called for it and the afternoon air was cold and crisp.

"I'd love that. But I have something I'd like to do first, if you don't mind."

"What is it?"

She tugged at the collar of my coat. "It's a surprise!"

"Well, then I can't honestly tell you if I mind," I teased. I couldn't imagine a single thing I'd mind doing as long as I was with her. Even if she suggested something as outrageous as ice skating, which was definitely at the top of the list of things I suspected she'd be interested in.

"Are you trying to wind me up?" She wrinkled her nose, and it looked so adorable I nearly had to kiss it.

Somehow I resisted the temptation, but just barely. "I am. Of course I don't mind. Take me where you will."

"Good because I already bought us tickets. Give me a second." She pulled out her mobile and made a few swipes. Then she slipped her arm through mine and tugged me toward the stairs. "This way. Our Uber will be here in five."

Less than twenty minutes later, we'd gotten in our car, crossed the Thames, and had been dropped off in front of Jubilee Gardens. There were many things around here that required tickets, but one option was especially obvious.

"We're going on the London Eye?" I asked nodding up at the cantilevered observation wheel in front of us.

"Yes! Have you ever been?"

"Not in years." Ellen and I had been newlyweds when it had opened. We'd come in the summer and it was hot and the queue had been long, but the thrill of floating more than four hundred feet about the river with my bride at my side had been unforgettable. All of London had been stretched out before us, and it had felt symbolic of our lives.

I'd come again with Aaron soon after my divorce, and the magic of the first time was nowhere to be found. He'd only been seven, and the view only interested him for about five minutes before he was ready for it to be over so we could go play at the playground. I'd been irritated and impatient and unimpressed. The whole thing had felt like an overpriced, overlong ferris wheel ride, and I'd vowed to never go on the bloody contraption again.

"Want to go again? With me?" Her eyes were big and intense as she stared at me for my answer.

"Yes. I do."

We made our way down the sidewalk toward the Queen's Walk and found the queue for the flexi tickets she'd bought. There were about fifty or so people ahead of us and the young lady who scanned Audrey's mobile to let us in said it would probably only be ten to fifteen minutes before we could get on.

"I thought about getting the fast pass," Audrey said as we waited. "But I didn't know what time we'd be done at the Gallery. I'm glad I didn't since it doesn't look like we'll need it. I'd expected it to be more crowded for being in the So Many Children and Tourists part of town."

I chuckled at her reference to the stereotypes map she'd used to familiarize herself with London. "It's not the season for tourists or children. You should see this place in the summer months. On second thought, you shouldn't. This is much better. Though clear skies would be ideal."

She looked up at the clouds, as though she hadn't noticed them before. "I would have thought you were a fan of this broody, gray weather."

"Oh, I am. But it doesn't do well for visibility."

"No visibility is a plus as far as I'm concerned."

"The whole point of this wheel is the views."

"I know, but I'm afraid of heights."

Somehow I'd forgotten this fact, or really never believed it in the first place. It was still so odd to think of her frightened of anything. But if she insisted… "Then why are we doing this?"

"Because I'm afraid of heights." She laughed at my

confused expression. "Fear is so annoying. It keeps people from doing and having things they might really want. It's usually stupid and unwarranted, too, the things that scare us. I know I'm not going to fall out of the sky. I know it, and yet my heart starts pounding, and I start sweating when I even think about going up there. Look at my hands!" She held out her palms for me to see. "Sweaty."

She stuffed her hands into her coat pockets. "But the London Eye is one of the most famous tourist attractions in London. I don't want to tell people back home I never rode because I was too scared. I'd rather face the fear head-on. Personally, I think it's the better way to live."

She was right. Of course she was right. And still I felt like arguing for some reason. "Facing your fears makes for a good life, yes, but that only works when you really don't want to be afraid any longer. It's possible that some people like to stay afraid."

"Why would anyone want to stay afraid?"

"I don't know. Because it's familiar, I suppose. You already know what to guard yourself from. You have all your safety nets set in place. And when you get over those fears, you open yourself up to becoming afraid of something else. Sometimes it's easier to live with the fears you know." This speech had come too easily to me. As though it was something I'd said before or was already formed inside me, waiting for a chance to be spoken.

She pressed her lips together tightly. "Well, that's just silly. I think holding onto fears makes it *easier* to be afraid of new things, not the other way around. It's like wagon wheels in a rut—once you've trained your neural pathways to react with anxiety about one thing, it isn't long before a lot of things scare you. I can't imagine living like that. Is it even living at all?"

I didn't want to answer, so I just shrugged. It seemed like a pointed question, like she was trying to confront me about my fears and how I lived my life—or *didn't* live my life, according to her.

Or maybe she hadn't meant it personally, and I just took it that way. I considered asking outright, but in the end, I was a coward.

"I do know this," I said genuinely. "You're a brave woman, Audrey Lind." Certainly she was braver than me. About all sorts of things.

The queue moved fast as the ticket attendant had assured, and we were led into a capsule shortly with nearly two dozen other people. That was one of the admirable features of the Eye's boarding process—though it was a popular attraction, the actual ride wasn't ever crowded. It would have been near untolerable to be stuck for thirty minutes on the wheel otherwise, even with the air conditioning.

I stepped in after Audrey who walked immediately to a spot against the window. "There's a bench here," I pointed out. "If you'd rather have some distance between you and the glass."

She shook her head. "This is good for now. I find it's better to dive right into these kinds of things. Tiptoeing around the fear only makes it worse."

"That it does." I moved next to her, placing my hands on the rail like she had done. The ride was already in motion, another one of its highlights. The wheel rarely stopped, even as passengers got on and off, making for one smooth trip.

But that also meant we were already rising, already climbing higher in the sky.

"Are you doing okay?" I asked. Audrey was feeling the anxiety of it. I could hear her shallow breaths and her knuckles were white as they gripped the railing.

"Fine," she said, her voice tight and high. "I'll be fine."

Though the clouds covered the sky, there was still a lot to see. Big Ben, Westminster Abbey, the Shard, but I was more interested in watching Audrey, looking for any cue she might give for help.

Not that there was much I could do for her now that we were in the air. I did my best to distract her, giving her the history of the wheel and offering tidbits of trivia about the city below us.

She didn't say anything, only blinked and nodded. Her gaze never moved, as though she'd anchored her eyes to some landmark below and was clutching on for dear life. There was something oddly inspiring about watching her. Her delicate throat swallowed. Her lip quivered. She reminded me of the Mark Twain quote that said something about courage being the master of fear and not the absence of fear.

Audrey was definitely afraid, and as awed as I was by her, I also felt helpless. And that made me terrified. It was how I often felt watching Aaron grow up and embark on scary new adventures. I knew he had to experience both the good and the bad to learn, that I couldn't intervene and learn for him. It was one of the hardest things to do as a parent, stand by and let this person I loved go through something trying.

It was just as hard watching Audrey. Not necessarily watching her on the wheel, but in her life. I wanted to wrap her in my arms and keep her safe from everything and everyone. Wanted to make sure she had every happiness, but I couldn't hand her the romantic, unambiguous future wrapped in a bow that she wanted. I had to let her get to her ending on her own.

It was a good thing she was courageous. It made it easier. For me, anyway.

"We're at the top now," I said encouragingly. "Look! You've done it! Gone to the top of the London Eye. It's all down from here."

She closed her eyes and let out a long deep sigh. Then she turned and rested her elbows on the rail behind her. "That's better."

I peered over my shoulder, following her sight lines. There was a small family speaking in Korean and snapping pictures in front of the opposite window, blocking Audrey's view. "You can't see a single thing this way."

She grinned. "Just how I want it. I told you—it's not about seeing anything."

A memory of the apartment hunting with her the first week we'd met popped into my mind. "You'd said you were afraid of heights before, but you didn't seem all that frightened by the windows in the New York flat."

"Because when we were there together, I was preoccupied with other things, if you remember. It's hard to be worried about your fears when you're on the verge of orgasm." Her eyes twinkled as she glanced at me, checking out my reaction. Trying to wind me up, most likely.

It was definitely working.

"Maybe that's what would make this better—if you got under my skirt." Her voice was low now, so that there was no way anyone could hear but me. "I could turn back to the window, and you could come right behind me, embracing me. You could hitch up my skirt, push my panties aside, stick your cock inside me. Make me feel real good. Distract me from the fall. I'm already wet from talking about it. You'd slip right in. Too bad we didn't book a private ride."

Such a fucking tease. I was instantly hard.

I put my hand around her shoulder and swiftly pulled her closer so I could whisper greedily into her ear. "I'm going to finger-fuck you under the table at dinner, I'm warning you now. Three fingers, deep and merciless, until you're shivering and boneless."

She turned her face so her mouth was inches from mine. "And then later, will you meet me in the bathroom so you can do me in a stall?"

Damn, she was perfect. Sensual and sassy and smart and strong. I could write books about all the amazing things she was. I could write sequels about all the amazing things she made me feel, and in that moment I was drowning in the awe of her. I was grasping for something to hold onto, gasping for air, and it didn't matter what I knew I *should* do because all I could think about was how much I wanted her with me. Always.

"Why haven't you accepted the permanent position at the museum?" I asked pointedly.

Her smile faded, and she stepped out of my embrace. "How do you know about that?"

"Jana told me. Answer the question." I sounded harsh and demanding, and I hated myself for it, but I couldn't help it.

Her brow knitted as she crossed her arms defensively over her chest. "Why are you talking to my boss about me?" Her features shifted as she seemed to realize something. "It was *you*, wasn't it? You donated the money for the job. Jana admitted there was a single donor. Why would you do that for me?"

My mouth went dry and my mind raced to come up with the most convincing lie. "Because I believe in the arts," I stated defiantly. That sounded good.

She stuck out her chin. "That's not why."

"Because I believe in supporting young artists," I amended.

"Would you have supported *any* young artist, or just me?"

The capsule was descending at a slow even keel, but I felt like I was tumbling from space without a parachute. I didn't want the tables turned on me. I didn't want her examining my motives—I wanted her to explain her own.

"I know you personally," I said defiantly. "It makes sense to want to help out a friend."

"You wanted to help out a friend," she repeated, unconvinced. "You donated the amount of a full-time salary for a *friend*." Her gaze bore into me as though she were trying to see *into* me. As though she thought she could find the truth and pull it out of me with just a look.

"Yes. I'm generous like that." I stared back at her, refusing to back down. She maintained eye contact, just as stubborn as I was. Whatever she wanted me to say, I wasn't going to say it. Not only did I not know what she was looking for, but didn't she realize yet that I wasn't that brave?

The tension between us was so tautly strung, it became unbearable.

I looked away first, staring out at the winter evening. Snowflakes were beginning to fall, and they glistened in the harbor lights. It was surreal and beautiful and sad, too, for some reason.

"I don't know why it matters now," I said quietly to the cold glass. "It doesn't seem you want the help, since you aren't choosing to take it."

"I haven't chosen to go either," she whispered, stepping into me. I could feel the heat radiating off her body, could feel it beckoning me closer.

I didn't move. "What are you waiting for?"

She turned toward the window, mirroring me. "A reason to stay."

I could give it to her, I thought. I wanted to give it to her, a reason to stay. I wanted to keep her and trap her and love her, selfishly. For me.

But...

But, but, but.

But that meant standing up to my fears. That meant possibly finding new fears. And it was easier to live with the fears I knew.

So instead of saying anything, I took the advice I'd given her and let her go.

CHAPTER
Fifteen

A CURTAIN CAME between us, brought down by my own hand. The countdown to the date Audrey was to accept or decline the job was foremost in my mind, and I hoped beyond hope that she'd decide to stay, but in the very real case that she didn't, I put up my walls. We still talked constantly. I spent the next several days with her, taking her around London, showing her my favorite parts of the town. We fucked nightly. Every morning she woke up next to me, but the increased time together was very superficial. I had to protect my heart. I kept her at arm's-length. I didn't let her in any more than she already was.

It was difficult at first, watching her flit around, preparing her wings for flight while I stayed tight and secure within my cage. I was familiar with the feeling of being tethered and bound. I'd been here before, and I dealt with it in the same way I had in the past. I closed down my emotions. I went numb.

I prepared to let her go.

Thursday night, four days to go on the countdown, I was just getting out of the shower when there was a knock on the door. I glanced at the time. Audrey was due to arrive in half an hour for our evening plans. She should have been off of work by now, but she'd said she needed to go home to get ready before coming over.

Dripping wet, with a towel wrapped around my waist, I checked the peephole. "You're early," I said as I opened the door.

My chest tightened when I really got a look at Audrey. She hadn't changed after work—she was still in tights and a jumper under her coat, the outfit she'd worn when I'd left her flat this morning. What concerned me, though, was her face. Her skin was splotchy, her eyes red and puffy, her makeup smeared. She'd been crying.

I went on alert. "What is it? What's wrong? What happened?" Whoever had hurt her, I had to know. I'd fix it. I'd hurt him back.

She shook her head dismissively. "I just had a bad day is all. Do you mind if we cancel the theater? I know you already got tickets, but I don't really feel like sitting through something right now."

"Don't worry about the show. Do you want to go somewhere else? Anywhere you want is fine with me. I'll even go ice skating, if that's what you'd prefer." The desperation to make her better was overwhelming.

"Can I just come in and maybe talk a little?"

"Of course, of course." I stepped aside for her to come in, then I opened my arms, expecting her to come in for an embrace.

Instead she stuffed her hands in her pockets and stepped away. "I don't really feel like being touched right now, if that's okay with you."

The rejection was unexpected and stung sharply. Was she upset with *me*?

Before I got too panicked about the possibility I talked myself down. I'd never seen her upset at all. Perhaps this was her usual method of coping.

"I'll…" I didn't know what to do. What I *should* do. She was standing in my entryway looking sullen and sad, and all I could do was stare at her. "Let me take your coat," I said finally.

"I'd rather keep it on for now, thank you. Could I maybe have some water?"

"Yes. Sure. I could put the kettle on, if you prefer."

"Water's fine."

She followed me into the kitchen and took a seat in one of the high chairs at the island. I grabbed a glass from the cabinet and filled it with water from the refrigerator then set it down in front of her.

I watched while she brought it to her lips and took a swallow. She was so quiet and pale. Not like her usual self at all. I yearned to wrap my arms around her and kiss her better. I couldn't stand seeing her like this, and not being able to touch her made me feel even worse.

"I hope I didn't pull you out of the shower," she said after a long silent minute, gesturing to the towel, loose at my hips.

"I was already getting out." It did feel awkward to be naked in front of her when she was like this. "Will you be okay for a minute while I throw some trousers on?"

She gave me a yes and a tight smile, and I took off to my bedroom in search of something to wear, but when I got there, I stood in the doorway for several seconds, thinking. My mind raced, imagining every scenario that would put Audrey in such a glum state. Something at work, probably. Or something back home? Was it Sabrina? Again, I wondered, was it me? I couldn't think of anything I'd done to offend her, but I was stuck to guessing, and didn't have many other ideas.

I wanted to *fix* it.

But I couldn't. I knew I couldn't. Even if I knew what was bothering her, I likely wouldn't be able to do anything but simply be there for her.

It was maddening.

With a frustrated sigh, I pushed myself into the task at hand, grabbing a pair of sweats from my dresser and hastily putting them on before returning to the kitchen.

She was where I'd left her, her coat still on, a classic beret beanie winter hat on her head. Ready to leave at a moment's notice. It distressed me—all of it, her posture, her unwillingness to share, her refusal to make herself comfortable.

I eyed the seat next to her, but moved around to the other side of the island instead. It was too tempting to touch her if I was close, and I needed to wait for her invitation.

Bracing my hands on the worktop behind me, I tilted my head and studied her with concern. "Do you want to talk about it? I know a compassionate nature isn't one of my better traits, but I assure you, I can listen."

She almost chuckled. Then she let out a long breath. "I just...I found out something today and it…" She shook her head, as though to erase her beginning. Then she started again. "I've decided to tell Jana that I'm not going to accept the job."

Her voice cracked, or my heart did. It felt suddenly hard to breathe. I'd seen this coming. I'd prepared. And yet, I wasn't ready.

I blinked several times, searching for a foothold on the ground that was quickly slipping out from underneath me. I wanted to demand she change her mind, but I had no place to. She *wanted* to stay, though. I could hear it in her tone.

"Is this why you're upset? If it's worked you up like this, then why go? You love your job. I know you do."

"I do. I do love it." Her brow furrowed. "But I love what I do. I can do it anywhere. I like the staff at the Gallery, but it's not like I've formed any real bonds there. This is the crossroads. This is when I decide what happens next in the bigger plan, and staying here is a big decision. It's planting roots. It's dealing with Visas and establishing myself here, and it's so far from Sabrina, and she's my only family left. It's one thing to go overseas and do something temporary, but it's not practical without…" She trailed off, disappearing into some private thought.

Audrey twisted her lip and stared absentmindedly at a spot on the island worktop. She was more in her head than in the room, and I longed to be there with her, but I waited for her to be ready to go on, not wanting to prod or poke while simultaneously wanting to shake her sharply and yell in her face to fuck practicality. My grip on the worktop behind me tightened as I held in my restraint, my nails digging into the underside of the silestone.

"I guess that's why I was so eager to try to find The Guy," she said eventually. "I know I said I'd let it go, and I have, but it would have made it easier to stay. I could justify everything I'd be losing with so much gained."

Her eyes reached for mine. "I really don't know why

I couldn't find him. It wasn't like I was being picky. I just wanted someone who would make me laugh. And challenge me. Is fun to be around. Gives good orgasms." She let out a quick laugh and then grew somber again. "Someone who thinks about me when I'm not with him. Someone I look up to, but doesn't make me feel small. Someone who takes care of me. Someone who puts me first. Someone who runs to me when I need him. Someone who just... loves me. Why is that so impossible to find?"

As she spoke, I could feel words forming inside of me, bubbling up within my chest, building toward explosion. They shaped in the back of my throat, they slid to the tip of my tongue, and no matter anymore if I believed them or that they weren't the words I wanted. They were solid and familiar, and they detonated with a roar. "You can't find it because it isn't real! None of it is. No one loves anyone more than themselves. Fate doesn't intervene to bring people together. True love is a fairy tale. It's a myth. Stop fooling yourself that it isn't and grow the fuck up!"

Audrey lifted her chin and fired back. "Or maybe I have found him but the man I'm in love with is a coward who has abandoned the possibility of anything good so he can be a cynic."

I already regretted my words. They'd come from a cold, shadowy place inside me, and I wanted to retract them and apologize immediately once they'd been said.

But now I was stunned into silence.

"Yes, it's you, you asshole. I'm in love with *you*." She'd never sworn before in my presence, and the word was a blunt display of how angry she was. How filled with frustration.

And still I couldn't say anything, could only stare at her with incredulity. She was *in love* with *me*? Impossible.

She was too smart for that. Too levelheaded to waste her heart on a shit like me.

"I know I told you I wouldn't fall for you," she continued. "Or I promised that I would try not to, and I *did* try. I thought I'd done a pretty good job of it, too, when we parted in New York. But then I saw you again here, and I think I realized then that I'd been in love with you from that very first kiss. But I knew you didn't want that. So I tried to be your friend. I tried to not think about you like that. I tried." She was worked up and animated, saying words that felt unimaginable and also plucked from my own head.

"But you went on those dates…" I was sorting it out. Slowly processing.

"I did! All those crappy dates, hoping I'd find someone else who'd make me forget you. I wasn't going to sit around believing that you'd change how you felt about love and marriage and babies for *me*. But then you'd do these things—stupid, wonderful things, like donate the money for my job and help me paint my freaking apartment—and I started to think *maybe*. Maybe something's there. And I didn't want to push, so I just nudged you when I could, and everytime I hit a brick wall, and so I'd back down because I knew you'd put it there for a reason."

She stood up suddenly, too agitated to stay sitting. "But then you know what I realized? I realized that you weren't behind that wall because you really thought life was better there. You were *hiding*. Because you're scared. And I get it. You don't want to be hurt, and I could be patient with that, because I think there's a part of you that really wants to come out. And I'm *not* Ellen. I wouldn't cheat. Ever. I'm fiercely loyal, and if you'd give me a chance to prove it…"

Her eyes sparked hot. "Except then! Then I find out today you went *on a date* with Jana, and maybe it's not fair, but that hurt. It hurt a lot, Dylan. It broke my heart, because you said that didn't interest you. And I believed you. Was that not true? Or is it just that you aren't interested in dating *me*? Because I can't believe that's the case. You feel something for me. You have to. I know you do. Don't you?"

She stared into me, her chest rising and falling with shallow, riled breaths, her cheeks pink with emotion. "Say something!"

There were so many things to say. I wanted to tell her that I *did* feel something for her. That Jana meant nothing. That I was deeply and hopelessly in love with her. That I could give her all those things she wanted. That I could be The Guy, the someone who ran to her and took care of her and put her first. All I had to do was open the door to my cage and step out. I could taste the nearness to freedom, could feel it beckoning to me like sunshine streaming through the bars of my prison. Could vividly imagine taking flight with her in the sky.

But I'd hesitated too long.

"I guess that's my answer," she said, her eyes brimming. She spun on her heel and headed toward the door.

She was walking away. I didn't want her walking away, and that sprung me into action.

"No, Audrey." The house phone started ringing, but I ignored it to chase after her. "Wait. Please, wait."

She didn't turn around. "I can't talk to you right now," she said in a choked voice. "Answer your phone."

I didn't give a fuck about the bloody phone. She was at the door now, opening it with haste and slamming it shut, just as I got to it. Cursing, I opened it and called again to her as she jogged down the hall toward the lift.

Janice Morgan, my next door neighbor, stepped out of her flat with her two German shepherds, blocking my path.

I danced this way and that, trying to get around the threesome. Finally, I put my hands on her shoulders and scooted her out of the way.

"Mr. Locke!" she said sharply at my back.

I stopped to see if I'd hurt her in some way, but found her pinched expression was directed at my clothing—or lack thereof.

A glance back at Audrey told me I wasn't going to catch her in the lift, and I couldn't go running down the icy sidewalk with no shoes and no shirt.

"Bloody hell," I muttered, turning back to my flat. I opened the cupboard next to the front door and pulled out a coat and slipped on a pair of loafers. Then I grabbed my mobile and my wallet (in case I needed to catch a cab and go directly to her house) and renewed my pursuit.

I took the stairs, pulling up Audrey's number on my phone as I raced down. It rang three times before her outgoing message picked up.

"Fuck." I tried again. This time it went immediately to her voicemail. She was avoiding me. I redialed, ignoring the annoyed look of the doorman as I blustered past him to the street. When the buoyant sound of her recorded voice filled my ear, I left a message. "Audrey, pick up. Ring me. Let's talk. Please."

Outside, I searched in both directions, trying to guess if she'd gone toward the underground station, and if so, which one, since I lived squarely between two. I couldn't see her either way so I scanned instead for a cab. None were in sight.

I picked a direction and started walking, typing out a

text as I walked.

DYLAN: You surprised me. That's all.

An incoming call interrupted my message, but I cursed when I saw Ellen's name instead of Audrey's. I sent my ex to voicemail and was about to go back to typing when I heard a car. I looked up to see it was a cab. Too late, I reached out to summon it and let out another string of swearing when it drove on by.

I went back to my message. Please come back. Please let me tell you everything in my heart.

I pushed SEND as my mobile vibrated with another call. Ellen, again.

"Jesus, what?" I roared.

"Dylan, I'm at the hospital. You have to come. It's Aaron."

CHAPTER
Sixteen

I MOVED IN a fog back into my flat. Thoughts raced through my mind, but I couldn't grasp any of them, like they were on the Autobahn and I was a pedestrian standing on the side of the road, watching them fly by. Simple words and phrases sped by like fuzzy blobs, the emotions and meanings impossible to fully comprehend: *Infection. Pain. It's serious. Hurry.*

There was only one thing I could cling to, letting it drive me through the haze—*get to New York. Get to my son.*

The next half hour was spent on the phone. With my assistant, mainly. She took over the major task of booking me on the next flight over the pond and arranging a car both to take me to Heathrow and another to pick me up at LaGuardia. Next, I talked to Amy, putting the reins of the company in her hands until who knew when. A call to Donovan followed, apprising him of the situation. Finally, my mother, who cried even when I assured her it was too soon to panic.

It was a lie anyway. If it were really too soon to panic, Ellen wouldn't have said I should come. But I couldn't think about that right now. I could barely think at all.

I didn't pack a bag. Even if I didn't have clothes and essentials in my New York apartment, I would have left empty-handed. My flight took off too soon—I was going to be scrambling through security to make it as it was—and I wouldn't have been able to concentrate on what I needed, what I didn't need. I had no idea how long I'd be gone. I was barely thinking clearly enough to remember to grab my passport.

I was in the cab on my way to the airport before I could identify the one thing I *did* need—Audrey. I was devastated when I got her voicemail again and was sure she hadn't turned her phone back on, but I tried over and over, hanging up each time the recording was finished. It was comforting to hear her voice, even if all she said was *I'm obviously not available or I'm avoiding you. If you don't leave a message after the tone, you'll never find out which.*

Finally, when I was checked in and boarded, I left a brief message telling her what was going on. Then I typed out a text, knowing she'd see it sooner.

DYLAN: Aaron has a serious infection and is in hospital. I'm about to take off to the U.S. now. Please, call. I need you. I need to tell you

I stared at the screen, trying to figure out what I needed to tell her.

Everything. That's what. Every bloody thing I'd never told her. That I loved her. That I wanted her. That I wanted to talk this through.

It was too much of a declaration over message. I deleted the last lines and ended with `Please, call`.

Then I put the phone on airplane mode and buckled in for the eight-hour flight.

There was a lot of time to think in the air, without internet connection. I thought about Aaron, of course, replaying Ellen's words in my mind.

"I took him into the clinic yesterday because he was complaining that his face hurt," she'd said. "They diagnosed him with a sinus infection and gave us antibiotics. His upper lip was a little bit swollen when he went to bed. When he woke up today, he was in a lot of pain and the swelling had spread down to his chin and up to the middle of his cheeks. I called the doctor again, and they said to take him to the E.R. They admitted him immediately, and Dylan, it's serious. You have to hurry and get here. He's getting an MRI now so they can try to determine the cause, and they're putting him on IV antibiotics and pain meds, but if they don't stop the infection, if the swelling moves past his eyes and to his brain..."

She hadn't finished her sentence, but she hadn't needed to. I understood clearly what she was saying even without hearing the words.

I didn't like thinking about that for too long, but almost every time I batted the thought aside, it immediately returned to buzz in my brain like an unwanted fly. The few times I managed to shoo it away for any significant amount of time, my head was filled instead with Audrey. Beautiful Audrey. Sweet, saucy Audrey. Bold and unafraid Audrey. Owner-of-my-heart Audrey. What to do about Audrey?

I never made it beyond the past. I retraced every step of our relationship, every encounter, every fragment of conversation I could recall. I saw her in her underthings, standing in front of the windows in my New York flat. I heard her humming as she painted her bedroom walls. I felt the pit in my stomach as she called me a coward. I watched her running out my door, two steps ahead of me, leaving me behind.

If Ellen hadn't called, I would have gone to her place and waited on her doorstep until she let me in. I could picture that far, but what happened when I saw her, what I said, what I did—that was beyond my imagination. I didn't know what to do about Audrey, and with Aaron tied up to a hospital IV in another country, it was impossible to consider seriously.

It was just after midnight when I landed at LaGuardia, and my mobile was dead. I hadn't thought to grab a charger, and while it was possible there might be one for sale in the airport, I was too eager to get to hospital. Asking Ellen for an update on Aaron could wait until then, and if Audrey had called, I wasn't sure I wanted to know. My priority right now had to be my son. I didn't have room for distractions, as sweet as that particular distraction might be.

The ride into the city was smooth and quick, a benefit of my late arrival. There weren't too many cars, and the warm front the region was experiencing after the prior week's snow had cleared up any lingering ice from the roads.

Getting past hospital security was a lengthier process. Visiting hours were over, and even though there were exceptions for minors, I couldn't ring Ellen to approve my relation to Aaron without my mobile phone. The main entrance was closed and the only way in was through the ER, which was filled with the typical late-night medical emergencies. It took more than thirty minutes to find someone who had the time to talk to me, but eventually I was given a pass and sent to the children's ward. Then there was another door to be buzzed through and a paper to sign at the Pediatric desk, but finally, I was directed to my son's room.

The door was ajar, and I stood outside it for a moment to catch my breath, then pushed it open. The lights were dim, and a curtain hid the bed where, I presumed, Aaron was sleeping. I'd expected to find Ellen stretched out in the recliner next to him, but instead, she was standing just inside the room with her arms crossed over her chest while she talked to a man in a lab coat.

"Oh, good. You're here," my ex-wife said quietly when I walked in. Her voice sounded a bit raspier than usual, and her eyes looked heavy and tired, but otherwise, she seemed as she always did—poised, collected. Cold. Clinical.

There had been a part of me that had wanted to reach for her the minute I saw her. While we spent most of our interactions these days in battle mode, none of our fights felt relevant at the moment. She was the mother of my child, a woman I still loved fiercely for that reason alone. There was no one who could better know what I was feeling, how distressed and out of my mind with worry.

But even with the man next to her, she seemed too detached for an embrace. Too withdrawn. It reminded me vividly of a night long ago, another cold night spent in hospital fretting over a child. *Her* child. Amanda hadn't made it through that night, and Ellen had shut down the minute her daughter's time of death had been declared. She'd become unapproachable. Distant. Aloof. It had felt impossible to try to comfort her.

I'd resented her for that then, and that resentment was

a barrier around her now, preventing me from pulling her into my arms.

"He's sleeping right now," she said, before I could ask. "This is Dr. Sharma. Aaron's going into surgery tomorrow morning, and Dr. Sharma's associate is to be the surgeon."

I shook the doctor's hand. He had a firm grip, and that reassured me for some reason. "I'm Dylan, Aaron's father. I'm sorry I don't know what's going on—I just arrived from London. Could you possibly get me up to speed? About everything."

"Yes, Mr. Locke. I'm sorry to meet you under such serious circumstances. I was actually only hanging around to update you."

My chest constricted like it had been gripped with a large hand, squeezing all the air out of my lungs. It hadn't even occurred to me that medical doctors didn't usually visit patients in the middle of the night until he'd said something. If he'd been waiting this late specifically to update me, then Aaron's condition had to have taken a turn for the worse.

Ellen read the panic on my face. "No, no, it's not what you think. Donovan hired Dr. Sharma to be available when you arrived. He knew you'd want to talk to a medical professional directly."

Bless Donovan Kincaid. Sometimes his overreaching really was appreciated.

Dr. Sharma explained to me the situation in detail. The MRI they'd conducted while I was in flight indicated that he had a dental abscess, and the infection had moved to his skin. "It's called cellulitis and is mainly treated by heavy antibiotics. Unfortunately, it's difficult to get the medicine exactly where we need it. The veins in the face are small, and it can take some time before the IV meds get into that area. The surgeon will scrape out as much of the infection as possible tomorrow morning, which should help speed up the process, but the most important component for fighting this is the antibiotics."

"They've already changed which antibiotic they were giving him once since this morning," Ellen added.

I didn't like the implications of that. "What was the reasoning for the change? It's been less than twenty-four hours. Surely that couldn't have been enough time to determine the first medicine wasn't working."

"It's not as concerning as it sounds," Dr. Sharma assured me. "We put him on one antibiotic when he checked in, and after watching him for a few hours and seeing the infection was spreading at a faster rate than we'd originally suspected, we decided to move him to a more powerful medicine."

"It's spread?" I sounded more alarmed than I wanted to.

Ellen met my worried gaze. "It's just under his eyes now, Dylan. And it's moving down his neck."

"That's bad, isn't it? You don't want it to move past his eyes." I was only repeating the information she'd given me earlier.

"That is correct, Mr. Locke. Once the infection gets past the orbital bone, it can easily enter the brain. Encephalitis is quite serious, but I don't want to worry about that until it reaches that point."

"And if it gets into his lymph nodes. That's bad too." Ellen wanted me to know all the worst-case scenarios, it seemed.

I appreciated this. I'd spent most of the flight imagining what they could be. I needed to know what the reality was. "What happens if it gets into his lymph nodes?" I asked.

"The lymph nodes can easily deliver the infection through the bloodstream, spreading the bacteria throughout the body. There is a possibility that could lead to sepsis."

The vice grip around my chest tightened. "Aunt Edna died of sepsis."

"That's exactly what I thought," Ellen said. Her lip trembled, the only indication of the desperate emotions that had to be raging inside her.

Dr. Sharma tried to soothe us. "Again, that's not something we should worry about until necessary. Right now we have a clear path of attack. Let's give the antibiotics time to work."

I thanked the doctor for his time and for staying so late and giving us reassurance. The minute he left the room, though, the anxiety of the possibilities pressed heavier on my shoulders. I caught Ellen's eye. Her features were smooth, but I knew her well enough to see the agitation simmering underneath. She was still closed off, her arms wrapped around herself. Nothing about her posture was inviting.

But I pulled her into my arms and clung to her anyway, something I maybe should have done more of when her child had died, because this time it was also *my* child, and I needed *her*, even if she didn't need me.

She didn't pull away, and after a while, I could feel her body soften in my embrace. We stood there for a long time, talking to each other only through touch, sharing the weight of this hardship as well as we could. When she finally broke away, her eyes were brimming, and she excused herself to go to the ensuite bathroom.

Alone, I took a beat to get myself together. Then I stepped around the curtain to see my son. He was sleeping on his back, his body twisted as though he wanted to be on his side, but couldn't manage it with the various hookups to machines. Or possibly, the pressure of laying that way hurt too much, which was understandable. His entire face, from his eye sockets down, was swollen. Much more swollen than I'd imagined. I couldn't even tell where his cheekbones were. Even his nose was misshaped with edema. He looked like a puffed-up marshmallow, and I didn't doubt he was in incredible pain.

I stood over him and gripped the bedrail until my knuckles were white. He looked so small and fragile, and I suddenly remembered standing over Amanda's bed. Remembered how she'd seemed small and fragile. Remembered how much it hurt to watch her slip away from this life and into the next.

It had been unbearable, really.

More unbearable than all the things that happened next—Ellen's complete shutdown, her string of affairs, our divorce. Amanda had been thirteen when I'd married her mother, and six years later, when she'd sat on her deathbed, I'd grown to love her as though she were my own. Losing her had ripped me apart. It had destroyed parts of me that could never be recovered. It was her death, not the end of my marriage, that had taught me the lesson I held onto so resolutely now—*love leads to loss.*

And I never wanted to feel that kind of loss again. If Aaron died…if he was no longer in my world…

A sob escaped from my throat.

I couldn't lose him. I wouldn't. Whatever I had to do, whatever I had to pay, Aaron had to stay alive. He was lodged inside me so deeply, that I was sure I couldn't exist without him. I was helpless at his side, but I silently vowed to do anything within my power to keep him here.

And I renewed an older vow too, the vow I'd made when I closed down my heart after Amanda—*never let anyone else inside*. No one. Not even Audrey. She'd worked her way past my walls, but not all of them, not yet, and it couldn't be too late to build more. If I didn't let Audrey in any farther than she already was, if I pushed her out of my heart all together, then there would be less chance that I'd ever be here again, standing on the brink of sanity while my world crumbled to pieces in front of me.

Losing her now would hurt, yes, but not like it could. Not like the possibility of losing Aaron hurt. Not like it would hurt if I let myself love her—*really* love her—and *then* lost her.

So I wouldn't love her. Not *really* love her. Or anyone, ever again.

Sure, it was a cruel, cynical way to live, but as far as I was concerned, it was the only way to survive.

CHAPTER
Seventeen

THE REST OF the night crept by slowly. I parked myself in a steel-framed upholstered chair while Ellen curled up in a lounger that converted to a bed. The room was dim, only a small light shone from a lamp next to the bed, but neither of us bothered to try to sleep. We knew it would be impossible.

For much of the time, we sat silently, listening to the chirps of the automated equipment hooked up to our son. I was thankful for the quiet, too weighed down with the enormity of the situation to manage an abundance of conversation. Even my thoughts were sparse and scattered. I thought about the milk container I left on the kitchen worktop and the Christmas gifts I had for my mother that I hadn't bothered to send off and impressed myself by remembering the song order of all the Metallica CDs I'd listened to in high school. Trivial things. Things that didn't have an emotional residue. Things that didn't make me want to find the nearest stairwell and scream until my voice gave out.

I imagined Ellen was in a similar fog. When she did

make the effort to engage, her statements were just as random. "The green in that painting reminds me of the shag carpet in your flat in Southampton," she said once. And another time, "I still haven't finished reading the *Outlander* series. I should get on that."

Each instance, I murmured something appropriate and meaningless and soon we'd fall back into taciturnity. The long stretches of silence were familiar and comfortable. We'd done this before—existed in separate cocoons of shared grief. This was something we knew how to do well.

"I have to remember to cancel my appointment with the internet company later today," she said just a little past four in the morning.

I blinked a couple of times, processing the simple statement. It was the kind of thing that didn't require a response, but I was beginning to bore of the stupor and this felt like a safe, mindless conversation to embark on. "Do you have a problem with your service?"

"I've had a terrible time with our old provider. Aaron complains every day when he tries to do his homework that he can't get the sites he needs to load."

I hmphed. "Sites he *needs*? Or YouTube videos?"

"I know, right? Though, it's both, I'm sure. So much of the education at his school is provided in other learning formats such as video and podcasts. I like it. I just swear the internet company is throttling download speeds. It's gotten progressively worse over this year. The irritating part is that it will be another three weeks before I can get a new appointment, even on a wait list."

I scowled at the annoyance she must feel. "Don't you have someone who can meet them for you? Aaron is always telling me that you're dating. Is there no one?"

"No one significant. No one who would meet the cable guy for me, anyway. No one who would come sit at the hospital with me while my son is in surgery."

We'd been conversing without eye contact, but now I turned my head toward her. "*I'm* here."

"For Aaron."

"And for you." I was grateful that I wasn't sitting at his bedside alone, and assumed she'd felt the same. It was a typical problem from our past—I assumed too much when I should have tried harder to really communicate.

I assumed too much about people in general.

I decided to make the effort now. "I mean that, Ellen. You're the only person who gets what I feel about him."

She looked at me while she considered. "No one can love your creation as much as you do except a co-creator, I suppose."

I started to nod in agreement, then thought about it more. "Although...I really loved Amanda."

Her eyes widened, surprised, perhaps, by the declaration. When she turned away, she wrapped her arms tighter around herself, and I knew I'd taken a wrong turn.

"I'll ring Donovan later," I said, steering us back to safer topics. "He can get someone over to your apartment to meet the technician."

"Thank you." She stared at an unidentifiable spot before her, and I figured she'd slipped back into a daze. Then, abruptly, she asked, "How about you? Do you have anyone you're dating?"

The question felt shocking, like a bucket of ice cold water thrown over my head. It was too close to talking about Audrey—*thinking* about Audrey—and I didn't want to do that.

But not answering all together would only draw more attention to the topic, so I responded with succinct honesty. "Not really. I don't do that sort of thing anymore."

Ellen shifted again to study me. "You don't do *what*? Have sex? Spend time in other people's company?"

I glanced quickly at Aaron. He was still sleeping, but I lowered my voice anyway. "My bed isn't cold. But I've found it's...easier...to live without any unnecessary attachments."

She let out a sigh laced with pity. "Oh, Dylan. When did you become so bitter? Did *I* do that? That's an awful lot of power to give me."

I frowned. I didn't like how it felt like she was turning the tables on what really happened. As though it were my fault that I'd loved her enough to be affected by her infidelity. "I'm not sure I'm comfortable discussing this with you," I said, hopefully putting an end to the matter.

"That's too bad. There was a time you'd tell me anything. I don't expect you to anymore, of course, not after... well. It's just sad to hear that you don't have someone in your life now. I always saw you as a man who needed to love to be alive. I never imagined you'd become so hardhearted."

"I was also very young when we met. Now I've grown up."

We fell back into silence then for the bulk of the next hour, until the commotion of shift change stirred us again. A nurse came in, turning on the overhead before he introduced himself.

At the light and the sound of the new, louder voice, Aaron shifted in his bed. "Dad? You're here. It's not

Christmas already, is it?"

I took the two steps to his side and leaned down over him, taking his hand in mine. "Hi, kid. Not Christmas yet. I came early. Flew all night. Boy are my arms tired."

He smiled then let out a groan. "Ow. It hurts to smile."

"It was a terrible joke anyway."

"A dad joke for sure."

My grip on his hand tightened. He was hurting, and there was nothing I could do about it. Parental helplessness: one of the worst feelings in the world. I would carry all his burdens for him if I could. I'd suffer all his pain.

"I'm okay, Dad," he said, as though I were the one who needed soothing. "I mean, I feel like I'm dying, but I'm okay."

My heart pinched. He was a far cry from death, but the possibility lurked too close for comfort, and if I continued to stand there and think about it, I was going to lose it in front of him.

Thank God the nurse stepped in to take his vitals, giving me a reason to step away. And then it was time to prepare for surgery. A slew of doctors and nurses came through in turns, discussing anesthesia and Aaron's allergies, administering new IV's and inspecting the extent of his swelling.

Another hour of this and then his entire bed was wheeled away, leaving Ellen and me alone to wait.

"Do you want any coffee?" I asked, needing something to do besides worry.

"I'm good. The machine out there is terrible."

"Oh." I didn't really want coffee anyway. I only wanted this whole nightmare to be over.

"Remember the last time he had anesthesia?" Ellen said when I didn't get up to leave. "After his adenoid surgery. He took forever to wake up."

"I remember. And those faces he made while we were trying to rouse him. Those were the funniest expressions I've ever seen on a human."

"He's always made those faces in his sleep. Since he was born."

I chuckled. "And the sounds he makes. He snores like he's an old man."

"At least that improved after the adenoid removal. It was nearly impossible to be in a room with him while he slept before that."

We exchanged a smile. This was better than waiting in silence or sitting in the dark with our thoughts.

"Remember how he always moved the s's at the front of words to the end of the word?" Ellen asked. "Like _stop_. He always said _tops_. And he loved riding on the _leds_ instead of _sled_."

I'd forgotten that he'd done that. It used to delight us to no end.

"That stupid stuffed pig he had. What was its name?"

"Stumpy," I said, the name coming easily despite not having said it in years.

"That's right. He called it _Tumpys_."

"He loved the twinkle, twinkle _tars_." I smiled as it came back to me.

"He always said you were so marts. 'Daddy is so _marts_. You're only a little bit _marts_, Mommy.'"

I chuckled. "_Marts_. I forgot that one." God, I loved the

kid. "He's grown up to be very *marts* himself."

"Very," Ellen said with pride. "And sweet. A very sweet boy."

"Don't you mean a *weets* boy?"

She laughed, but it quickly faded. "Sweet, but never cuddly. I thought I'd done something wrong with him in the beginning because he never wanted me to hold him the way Amanda did."

I was taken aback. She'd never mentioned this fear when we'd been together. "That's just his personality. He's still not very touchy. How is that your fault?"

"I don't know. I wondered if it was because I wasn't as clingy to him as I had been with Amanda. He was a second child, and that is what it is, but I couldn't help feeling guilty about it. Aaron always slept in his crib, from the minute he came into the world, but Amanda was always in my bed. I remember the day she was born, holding her in my arms, wrapped up like a little burrito, and I just didn't want to let her go, even as I fell asleep. The nurse came in and asked if she could take her for me, put her in her bassinet at least, and I said no. I didn't want to let her go. I loved holding her."

"She was always an affectionate girl." It hurt to remember that, how warm Amanda had been. She had been nearly a teenager when I'd met her, but her biological father had never been in the picture, except to write a child support check every month. I'd quickly filled the spot of patriarch, even though I'd only been a dozen years older than her. Maybe she accepted me so easily *because* we were so close in age. I'd understood the girl better than the men her mother had dated that were closer to her own age. Ellen had always joked it was one of the perks of marrying a younger man, saying I bridged the culture gap between her and her teen.

Thinking about that made me think of Audrey and how she'd been so good at communicating with Aaron the couple of times they'd interacted.

But I didn't want to think about Audrey.

I wasn't so sure I wanted to keep thinking about Amanda, either. It was too painful. Yet, it was cathartic talking about her with Ellen. We'd waited too long to reminisce together about her, and it felt like progress between us, despite the emotions it drudged up.

"Remember how she always begged us to let her sleep with Aaron?" I asked. "I always felt so bad for saying no."

"He was a baby," Ellen laughed. "It was because she never liked to sleep alone. Remember how often she snuck in our bed? When she was really little, she used to sleep so close to me that I'd wake up and her head would be *on* my head. Like I was her pillow. I couldn't imagine how she found that comfortable."

"She was still doing that when I met her. We'd watch telly together, and she'd be fused into my side. She had zero personal boundaries. Anytime I had any food or drink, she'd take it without even asking. She truly believed in the 'mine is yours, yours is mine' philosophy of co-living."

"It was annoying sometimes."

"It was annoying a lot of the time," I agreed. "And also...also not." It was hard to look back at the nuisances, things she'd done that had been exasperating at the time when I'd give everything in my bank account to have her back and bothering me just one more time. Losing a child was the true definition of hell. The worst part was that it never went away. It burned and burned forever. Eternal damnation.

It was such serious pain that it made a person want to do anything to avoid feeling ever again.

"She looked up to you. So very much." Ellen's voice caught, and when I glanced over at her, I saw a tear rolling down her cheek.

I wiped at my own eyes. I couldn't do this anymore. I couldn't continue with this excruciating flood of emotions, remembering my dead stepdaughter, worrying about my ill son. "You know what? This isn't helping. Trips down memory lane are supposed to be bittersweet, but this feels more like a haunting. Like a visit from the Ghost of Christmas Past."

Ellen sat up and peered sharply in my direction. "If this is a haunting, I think I'm actually the Ghost of Christmas Future. Look at me. I've lost everything I've ever loved in this world. My parents. My daughter. Then you—the love of my life. And I'll never get those things back."

I was speechless. I'd been the love of her life? I'd believed that once upon a time, but she still felt that way?

"I'm alone now," she went on. "And lonely, with nothing and no one in my life but Aaron, and even if he does pull through this—"

"He's going to pull through this, Ellen," I interjected forcefully.

"*If and when* he pulls through this, I've got...what? Another handful of years before he goes off to college. What will I have in my life then?"

My scowl deepened. "Stop it. It's not too late for...I don't know, for anything you want. You're fifty-three. Not one hundred. You have a lot of life to look forward to." As much as I'd hated her at times, I'd also loved her. I'd hated her *because* I'd loved her so much. I still loved her in a way, and I sincerely wanted nothing but good things for her.

"A lot of life to look forward to *alone,* if I can't turn myself around." She settled back into her chair. "I know my issues, what I have to work through, but it's unbearable to me that you, of all people, might be following in my footsteps. Especially if I had anything to do with it, which I'm sure I did. Don't be *me,* Dylan. Don't stop getting attached. Let people into your heart. Cherish the love you have while you have it. Otherwise, what's the point in even living?"

It was a bloody conundrum. A catch twenty-two. Live a life with love and risk being destroyed. Live a life without and never really live. I thought I'd worked it out—earlier tonight, earlier in my life—but Ellen sparked something in me when she referred to me as the love of her life. I'd felt that way about her once, too. I certainly didn't feel that way anymore. I'd grown out of her. Grown past her.

And it struck me then that the loneliness that she talked about, familiar as it was, didn't accurately describe my current state of living. Sure, I'd been as miserable as she was now, living the same old bland routine with no color in my world. I'd walked through my life in a bubble, sealed off from any contamination of sorrow or happiness and joy and hope, and there had been no point.

But then Audrey had walked into my life and changed everything. She'd made me a better person. She'd made me happy and hopeful and now, without any promise of her in my future, I was back to being a wretched curmudgeon, and if I was honest with myself, I didn't feel safer from sorrow than I had with her at my side. In fact, she made me feel *more* protected from heartbreak.

She made the risks seem worth it. And selfishly, I

wanted her here with me now, comforting me. Reassuring me. Sitting by my side while my son went through surgery.

I wanted her with me after that too. I wanted her with me for always. And when I tried to think the phrase "love of my life," it was her face that popped up. Her eyes. Her laugh. Her everything. Why would I let her slip away? Why would I, as Ellen had said, give that much power to a miserable, lamentable past? Why would I not take every chance to avoid the future that she presented, a future that was sure to be my fate if I didn't make a change now?

I stood up suddenly and looked at the clock on the wall. It was just past seven in the morning. That meant afternoon in London. Audrey probably already told Jana she didn't want the job, but if I got to her in time, she could change her mind. I had to change her mind.

"What's wrong?" Ellen asked.

I pulled out my phone from my pocket and tried to turn it on before remembering it was dead. I kicked myself for not asking around earlier for a charger. "I need to make a call. Can I borrow your mobile?"

"Sure." She stood up and crossed to the small table where her mobile was charging. After tapping in the password, she handed it over. "Zero, seven, two, nine is the code if it locks up again."

The numbers were familiar. "Our anniversary?"

Her cheeks flushed. "It's memorable, that's all."

For the second time since I'd arrived, I pulled her into my arms, hugging her tight. So much had passed between us, so much good and so much bad, and I didn't regret any of it. I didn't even regret having loved her as deeply as I had. As I *still* did.

But it was finally time to move on. It was time to let

go of her and Amanda and all the hurts of the past that I'd held so tightly for so long. It was time to stop living so bloody scared.

I kissed her head before I pulled away. "I'm still here with you, don't doubt that for a second," I reassured her. "I'm just going to be out in the waiting room, making this call."

"Go," she said. "I'm going to pace the room, anyway. It's less embarrassing to do it when there's no one else around."

I didn't want to leave her alone, but I had to take care of this before it was too late, and while Aaron was in surgery was the best time to step away.

Without my own phone, it was harder to do what I needed. I didn't have Audrey's number memorized, and when I called the staff number listed for her department on the Gallery website, I was told she'd called off for the day.

I was sure she wasn't ill. She was likely upset, and I hated myself for being the one who'd caused that.

I had to get a hold of her.

Donovan would be able to get me her number. My thumb hovered over his name in Ellen's directory. Then I had another idea and dialed the number to my office instead.

"I need you to do something for me," I said when I'd been transferred to Amy's line and she'd answered.

"Dylan! How are you holding up? What's going on with Aaron?"

"He's fine. Or, not fine yet. He's in surgery, but I'm praying he's going to be fine, and that's not why I'm calling. I'll give you an update on him as soon as I have it.

I need something else in the meantime." I spoke rapidly, running my free hand through my hair as I paced the length of the waiting room.

"Uh, okay. What can I do?"

"I'm not sure exactly. Something big, but I'm not very good at this so I don't know quite what that is."

"This isn't something I can work with, Locke."

"Right, right." I tried to pull my frantic thoughts into something cohesive. "I need you to go to Audrey's for me. I'll give you the address. I need you to go over there with flowers and chocolates and...I don't know...balloons! Balloons are good. Heart-shaped balloons. And lots of flowers."

"I think you have the holidays mixed up. It's Christmas season, not Valentine's. I'm not sure I can find chocolates and heart-shaped balloons."

"Do the best you can, then. Get whatever you think might be romantic. The biggest romantic things you can find, and then tell her I love her. Tell her I don't want her to go, and that I love her, and that I'm not going to be scared anymore." I paused, wondering if there was something else to add, but couldn't think of anything. "Is that good? Do you think that's good? Do you think she'll think that's good?"

"I think she'll think that's quite wonderful. But she isn't home right now."

The voice wasn't Amy's, and it came from behind me, not from Ellen's phone. With the mobile still pressed to my ear, I turned around and suddenly the light in the room was brighter and my knees went weak and my heart was pounding like it would jump out of my chest.

Because there she was. There was Audrey. Bundled up

like an eskimo, her cheeks flushed, her eyes shining.

"Never mind," I told Amy, never taking my eyes off the woman in front of me. "Cancel it. Cancel all of it."

I ended the call without saying goodbye, and let the mobile slip out of my grasp to the carpet so I could have both hands free as I took Audrey into my arms.

She threw her hands around my neck and pulled my head down toward hers. My mouth found hers easily, like it was made for this, made to only kiss her. I kissed her like it had been decades since I'd last seen her. I kissed her like I hadn't been alive until now.

I kissed her like I would die if I didn't kiss her.

Breathless, I pressed my forehead against hers. "Stay in London. Let me be the reason you stay."

She nodded, tears sliding down her face. "Okay."

Then I kissed her again, like I'd never let her go.

CHAPTER
Eighteen

WITH MY ARMS still around her, I pulled back to look at her. The enormity of what she'd done for me struck me suddenly. She'd gotten on a plane, flown across an ocean at the drop of a dime. The price of the ticket alone had to be an obstacle. "I can't believe you came."

She pushed my chest lightly with her palm. "Of course I came. It's your son, you ninny." She searched my features, seemingly as in awe of me as I was of her at the moment. "Did you think I didn't really mean it when I said I loved you? As soon as I got your message, I had to be here."

My breath felt trapped inside my chest. She'd said the words before, but I hadn't been ready to hear them then. *Really* hear them. There was a great deal of things to say, things I should have said the first time she'd said them.

But I hadn't lost complete sight of where we were and what was going on. "Audrey, there are things I want to tell you, just…"

She cut me off with a shake of her head. "It can wait. What's going on with Aaron?"

"He's in surgery right now." Suddenly I remembered my ex-wife. "I need to go back to his room to wait for him."

"Do you want me to come with you? Do you want me to go? Whatever you need..."

I tightened my grip on her waist. "Don't go. I want you to stay. Please?"

"I want to stay, too. Thank you for letting me stay." She sounded relieved, and I almost laughed at how ridiculous it was that she wasn't sure that I'd want her with me, when I wanted her as acutely as I did.

I was so grateful, in fact, that I couldn't begin to tell her. I wasn't sure I could speak at all, actually. I cleared my throat. "Would you...may I introduce you to Ellen?"

Her lips turned up in a soft smile. "I'd like that."

I kissed her once more, quickly, simply because I couldn't *not* kiss her, then grabbed the phone off the floor and held it in one hand and Audrey's hand in the other as we walked to the hospital room. Along the way, I updated her on Aaron's condition telling her about the abscess and the swelling and the possibilities of encephalitis and sepsis. All of it sounded just as awful as it had when I'd heard it from Dr. Sharma, but somehow the situation seemed a little more hopeful, just because she was here.

At Aaron's room, I unexpectedly became nervous. I'd never introduced another woman to Ellen, and something about that felt significant. More significant, even, than introducing a woman to my mother.

I dropped Audrey's hand so I could go in first. "Um, Ellen..."

She was standing at the window, staring outside at the street below.

I waited for her to shake out of her thoughts before I went on. "I sort of lied earlier, when I said I wasn't dating anyone." I reached behind me and pulled Audrey to my side.

"Hi," she said, offering her free hand to Ellen before I could complete the introduction. "I'm Audrey."

Ellen's eyes went wide. She blinked a couple of times, a faint smile appearing on her face. She shook Audrey's hand. "Ellen Wallace."

"I'm very glad to meet you, though I'm so sorry it has to be under such terrible circumstances."

"Nice to meet you as well." She was surprised, I was sure, and why wouldn't she be? I'd given her no reason to see it coming. She narrowed her eyes and looked curiously in my direction. "Dylan, have you been hiding her from me?"

"No! No. Not at all." Though I was at a loss of what to say to explain our relationship.

Thank God Audrey was better at these things than I. "It's not his fault," she explained. "We've known each other for more than a year, but…" She looked at me, her cheeks pinking. "We're only just now sorting out what we are to each other."

God, she was perfect.

Ellen's forehead was still knotted in confusion. "Do you live here? Or in London?"

"I'm American, obviously," she giggled. "And we met here. But I've been living in London for the past several months. I flew out here as soon as I heard about Aaron.

Dylan didn't know I was coming."

Ellen's features relaxed. "Ah." She gave me a knowing look that I couldn't interpret. Not for lack of trying.

She returned her focus to Audrey. "Dylan has always had a thing for American girls."

"Really? I guess I never put that together. It works out, because I have a thing for this British man."

Now I was the one to blush.

It was time to change the subject. "Did you hear anything while I was gone?"

Ellen's sober expression returned. "Nothing yet. It should be soon. I hope. I'm going crazy with the waiting."

"I can't even imagine." Audrey's tone was genuinely sympathetic. A beat passed. "If you'll excuse me, I could use some tea. I spotted a coffee station in the waiting room. Can I bring you both something?"

Ellen declined, while I asked for Earl Grey, if they had it.

As soon as she left the room, my ex-wife smirked. "Dylan, you dog. I can't believe you didn't mention her. She's adorable."

"She's young." I was prodding her, trying to provoke her into admitting what she had to really be thinking.

Ellen just rolled her eyes. "*You're* young."

"She's *younger*." Maybe it was silly to expect my ex-wife to be shocked by the age difference, seeing as how she was ten years older than me.

It was probably even sillier that I worried about the gap at all. I loved Audrey exactly as she was, and for some insane reason, she loved me.

Ellen seemed to sense I needed more reassurance. "I'll tell you the same thing my mother said to me when I brought you home for the first time: Right on."

She winked, and anxiety rolled off my shoulders. "I've still got it," I said, boastfully, embracing the lightness of the moment, as fleeting as it might be. "It's probably because I'm in a band. She's an artist. She appreciates other artists."

Ellen full out laughed. "Oh, is that what she appreciates about you?" Her smile lingered. "Seriously, though. You have someone who will sit at the hospital with you. You better keep her."

That had been the knowing look she'd given me, I realized now.

"I'm working on that." I wasn't sure how I'd expected Ellen to react to me having a girlfriend—was that what Audrey was? I hadn't imagined bringing a woman around her since she'd cheated on me. Then, I'd fantasized an insane amount about the idea, about having a sexy, young, intelligent bombshell on my arm, about flaunting it in her face. I'd wanted to hurt her, make her jealous. Make her regret giving me up.

This was nothing like what I'd imagined. It was so much better.

A few minutes later, Audrey returned with the tea, then a few minutes after that, the shift nurse came in. "Mr. Locke, Ms. Wallace, I'm happy to report that Aaron is out of surgery. He's in the recovery room now. Would you like to be taken down to see him? The surgeon can talk to you both there."

"Yes," Ellen answered immediately.

"I'd like to go as well." We'd already been told only

parents were allowed in recovery. I knew Audrey would understand, but I looked at her for confirmation.

"I'll be here when you get back, if that's okay?"

I wasn't sure if she was asking me or the nurse. "Can she stay in the room while we're gone?"

"Sure. I'll bring another chair. And your relation is...?" The nurse studied Audrey, trying to find a resemblance, perhaps.

I waited for Audrey to play her usual game and claim to be my daughter or a niece, but she didn't. She reached out and took my hand. "I'm his girlfriend."

So she *was* my girlfriend.

I liked the sound of it, but also, it didn't feel right. It wasn't enough of a word to describe everything she was to me. Everything I wanted her to be.

But right now I needed to see my son. The rest could wait until later.

The procedure had gone well. Aaron would need a root canal and debridement once he got out of the hospital, but the surgeon was confident he'd gotten the bulk of the infection out. Now it was a matter of waiting for the IV antibiotics to take care of the rest. He expected we'd see progress within the next twenty-four hours or so.

Like the last time our son had undergone anesthesia, Aaron took a while rousing. It was nearly two hours later before he was ready to return to his floor. He was still fairly out of it as they wheeled him into the room, and I debated whether or not I should wait to re-introduce him to Audrey.

Turned out Aaron made the decision himself. "I know you," he said, looking Audrey over. "You're my dad's girl-friend, aren't you?"

I grinned over at the woman I loved. "Seems he figured it out faster than we did."

"I knew the minute we first met that you were a smart one," she said directly to Aaron. "I hope you don't mind that I'm here right now. I don't want to invade your family time."

"I don't mind. You're nice." His eyes closed. "And pretty," he added before drifting back to sleep.

I didn't say it out loud, but I had to agree. That kid re-ally was *marts*.

The rest of the day was spent at his bedside. Audrey became more than a comfort; she was also extremely help-ful. She brought us food when we got tired of the cafeteria options. Ellen gave her the keys to her apartment and Au-drey met the cable guy. She bought me a charger for my phone so I could distract myself with internet surfing. She engaged in idle conversation with each of us. She sat by my side.

Through it all it became more and more clear how much I needed her, how perfectly she fit into my world, how completely she belonged to me. And even as my main focus was my son and his illness, the wheels worked in the back of my mind. Ellen's advice played over and over on repeat—*you better keep her*. Little by little, I broke down what I'd have to do, what I'd have to become to make that happen. Little by little, I unraveled the knots that had previously been barriers to letting Audrey in permanently.

As evening approached, she encouraged me to consid-er some self-care. There had been no changes in Aaron's status, but no indication that it would worsen. Reluctantly, I left the hospital for the night. I was exhausted and needed a shower, a bed, a change of clothes. Audrey was just as tired. We collapsed into sleep as soon as we got to the flat.

We returned to hospital Saturday morning for a repeat of the prior day, with one difference—Aaron's swelling was receding. The latest antibiotic seemed to be working. It was easier to leave that night, and Sunday when we arrived at hospital, the doctor informed us that Aaron would be able to go home later in the day.

The news was so overwhelming, I lost it. I had to make an excuse to step out of the room so Aaron wouldn't see me overcome with emotion. Audrey followed, and I buried my head in her neck and sobbed with relief.

After the episode passed, my head was clearer, as though a long lying fog had finally lifted. The foolishness of the vows I'd made the first night at Aaron's bedside became apparent. Silently, I made new ones. I vowed to make Aaron my priority and to be the best father possible. The first step in doing that was to be the best man possible. Audrey made me that kind of man.

I slipped out again soon after to make another phone call.

"I need your help," I said to Donovan when he answered the line.

"It's about goddamned time."

Aaron was discharged a few hours later. Audrey and I helped get him home. He'd had several gifts sent by friends and family members while he'd been ill—flowers,

230 | LAURELIN PAIGE

balloons and the like. Too much for Ellen to manage by herself. I also wanted to personally see him back in his normal environment. Even though he went immediately to bed, it was reassuring to see him in his own room rather than the clinical surroundings of the hospital.

And I had reasons for not wanting to go back to my own apartment quite yet.

We stayed for dinner, delivery pizza at Aaron's request, and by late evening, I was finally ready to leave. I was more than ready, actually. There was nothing more I could do for my son. He was on the road to recovery. He was tucked in and medicated. He'd listened to me tell him I loved him countless times without protesting too much.

Now I turned my focus to the woman who'd sat patiently on the backburner throughout the ordeal. I wanted her. I needed her in a very different way than I had the past few days, and with the furtive glances she'd been giving me for much of the day, I was pretty sure she needed me in the same way.

By the time we walked out of Ellen's building to meet my car, the air around us was charged with arousal. My body felt too hot, even in the winter air. My fingers ached with the craving to touch.

The driver held the back door open while Audrey slid across the backseat of the saloon. Seeing there wasn't a window separating the front seat from the back, I turned to him before I got in myself. "I'm sorry for what's about to happen," I said.

Though I wasn't really *that* sorry.

Audrey was on the same wavelength. As soon as the door shut beside me, she crawled on top of me, straddling her legs over mine.

"This is familiar." I gripped her hips and pulled her pelvis forward so she could feel the thickening pressure of my cock beneath her. "Are you going to ask me for some sort of lessons now?"

She raised her chin so I could place open-mouthed kisses along her neck. "Actually, I'm going to give you a lesson."

"Color me intrigued." I slipped my hands inside her leggings and palmed her ass. My mouth found hers and I sucked on her bottom lip, making it plump and swollen.

When I went in to kiss her more completely, however, she pulled just out of reach. "Lesson time, Dylan."

I gave her a mock frown. I was eager for her lips, eager to taste her, eager for the talking to be over.

But I did enjoy the idea of reversing our usual roles. "All right, then, Ms. Lind. School me."

"You have been a bad boy, Dylan Locke."

"Yes, yes. A very bad boy."

"I'm here with you right now because I love you, but I almost wasn't here. You almost let me slip away. You almost lost me all together."

Oh. So this was a serious lesson then.

Except, the whole while she scolded me, Audrey rocked up and down along the length of my cock.

"I know, I know," I said, distracted by the fire she stoked in my lower regions. "I fucked up." I reached again for her lips.

Once again she darted away. "If you want to keep me with you, you can't play this scared routine anymore. I already called Jana and accepted the job at the Gallery, but you can't be closed off if you want me to really stay.

You can't keep building these walls. You have to tell me how you're feeling. You have to start trusting me with your heart. You hurt me, Dylan."

Guilt won over lust. I brushed her cheek with my knuckle. "I know, and I'm incredibly sorry. I never wanted to hurt you. If it helps, I hurt us both."

She cupped my face with her hands and lifted it toward hers. "It *doesn't* help. I don't like you hurting. I don't like either of us hurting. Don't do it again."

"I won't," I promised. But it came out on a groan as she drew a lazy circle over my crotch with her hips.

"I mean it." She drew another circle. Then a third.

My eyelids threatened to close from the agonizing sparks of pleasure shooting through my dick. "I can't tell if you're trying to punish me or please me."

"My favorite kind of punishment." She was such a vixen, that woman. Such a bloody tease.

She bent her forehead to mine as she continued to grind on my cock. "Tell me you understand what I'm asking from you."

"I understand."

"Promise me you're going to do better."

"I promise," I moaned.

"Promise that you aren't going to assume I'm going to be someone different than I am based on your experiences with other people."

"Audrey." I pulled her pelvis tight against me so her movements would still and I could concentrate for a moment. Then I looked her directly in the eyes. "I understand that I have been an incredibly daft wanker where you are concerned, that I hurt you, and that you are more mature than I could ever hope to be, and I vow on my very life that I will endeavor to be a man who deserves to have your love and affection for as long as I shall be allowed to receive it. Now, let me kiss you."

A grin broke out on her face as she brought her lips to mine. My mouth latched onto hers and held there, savoring the connection. I took my time with my tongue, licking into her with shallow strokes before fully stretching out to inhabit her completely. Her hands came up to tangle in my hair. Our breaths came rapid and synched. I bucked my hips to press against her, wishing she wasn't wearing trousers. Wishing she wasn't dressed at all.

With a soft moan, she tilted her head up, offering her neck. I licked along her the curve of her chin and nibbled down the exposed skin.

"Are we going to talk about what it means that you asked me to stay in London?" she asked, panting.

"No." My palms found her tits and squeezed them together. I was going to fuck her here. I hadn't done that yet, and I definitely needed to add it to my to-do list.

"No?" The sharpness in her tone forced me to give more attention to the question.

"I mean, yes. We will. But not right now." I leaned for her mouth, but she turned away so my kiss landed on the side of her lips. She wanted a more committed answer. "I promise we'll talk about it, Audrey. Soon."

She let me kiss her then, but it was brief. "Like, in Dylan-time soon? Or in regular-people-time soon?"

I had to chuckle at the necessity for the clarification. Still, I only responded with, "Soon."

"Sir? We're here." Something in the driver's tone suggested we might have been parked at the curb for several minutes. I hadn't even noticed the car had stopped moving.

Audrey and I broke apart. Immediately I felt cold without her warmth. I ushered her in through the lobby as quickly as I could. Once the doors were shut in the lift and we were alone again, I pushed her against the wall and pinned her hands behind her back.

My mouth hovered over hers. "I'm going to lick your pussy so long tonight, you won't have any sensation anymore by the time I'm done."

She whimpered.

"And then I'm going to fuck you. I'm going to fuck you everywhere. I'm going to fuck your mouth and your tits. I'm going to fuck your sweet cunt until you come so hard. You won't be able to stand tomorrow."

"Dylan…" she gasped. I cut her off with a greedy kiss.

The doors opened on our floor, and we were so into each other, they closed again before we were able to untangle ourselves. Laughing, I pushed the DOOR OPEN button. She darted out ahead of me, and I chased her like she was a bitch in heat, and I was the tramp that had caught her scent. At my flat, she stroked me through my trousers while I kissed her and dug in my coat pocket for my key. Finally, I had the lock undone and the door open.

"Don't turn on the lights," I said when I stood back to let her go in before me. Then I said a silent prayer that everything was as it should be inside.

I was still in the foyer when I heard her gasp. My pulse quickened. My heart hammered against my chest like it was trying to escape. Quickly, I hung up my coat in the cupboard and followed in after her.

The room had been beautifully transformed. I almost gasped as well. Rose petals had been scattered across the wood floor. Red and white poinsettias were strewn in bunches around the furniture. White electric tea lights and evergreen garland weaved through the plants and tangled up the small cart that had been wheeled in for the occasion. At the top, several electric candles glowed next to a silver champagne bucket. Two long-stemmed glasses were set next to it along with a tray of fresh strawberries.

Audrey's back faced me as she slowly took in every detail of the scene. I watched her reflection in the window. One hand was clapped over her heart, another over her mouth in awe. Her voice was quivering when she exclaimed, "This is so unbelievably romantic!"

It *was* very romantic. Donovan Kincaid was much better at this than I was, it seemed. I'd have to take notes.

Then she saw it.

I knew by the way her breath hitched, and her knees started to sway. She reached a shaky hand out to pick up the object from the arrangement on the cart, and when she turned around to me, she held it between her thumb and index finger, and I saw it too. It was as perfect as the image on Tiffany's website had indicated. The two carat round diamond sparkled with the candlelights and appeared to be floating in its setting above a radiant rose gold band.

I got down on my knee and reached my hand out to the sweet girl in front of me. To my surprise, she fell down on her knees with me. She slipped the ring on the first knuckle of her thumb and clutched onto my jumper.

"But you don't believe in commitment. You don't want a relationship," she said, tears streaming down her cheeks. Despite her words, her tone was hopeful. "You said…" She was too choked up to go on.

I cupped one hand against her face. "I'm a liar, Audrey.

I want a relationship. With you. I want it all with you. I am madly drowning in love for you. I have been since that first week in New York, I was just too chickenshit to admit it."

Her eyes widened. "Since then? Why didn't you…?"

She didn't have to finish the question for me to understand what she was asking. "I *couldn't* tell you. I could barely tell myself, at first, and when I figured it out, I couldn't bring myself to share that with you. I wanted you to be happy, and I was convinced I couldn't possibly be the person to give that to you."

Gently, I loosened her hand from my jumper so I could take the ring off her thumb. I held it up in between us, letting it be the underline for everything I had to tell her. "I've spent all this last year reminding myself of all the reasons why I'm not good for you, Audrey. But I never stopped to list all the reasons why *you're* good for *me*, and when I try, it's such an incredible job to even begin to catalog. The long and short of it, though, is that you make me a better man. You make me believe in things I never thought possible. You make me love when I thought I was no longer capable. You make me want a very different future than the one laid out for me at present."

I took her left hand in mine and eased the ring on the appropriate finger. It fit perfectly. Sabrina was to thank for that.

Audrey blinked at the diamond on her hand before peering up at me.

With my thumbs, I brushed tears off her face. "I'm beguiled by you, Audrey. And when you said you loved me, when you flew across an ocean to be at my side when I needed you most, a selfish hollow in my heart ached to believe that I might have something that I could give you, even if I could never balance the scale between us. Marry me and let me spend the rest of my life trying."

Her lips rolled inward as she tried to suppress a sob and she flapped her hand in front of her face, as though that would dry up her tears. Nodding profusely she managed to squeak out her response. "Yes. I say yes."

A wave of relief rolled through my shoulders. I hadn't realized how worried I'd been about her answer until I heard the one I so desperately wanted. "Thank God," I sighed. With my palms braced on each side of her face, I kissed her, and kissed her. Kissed her with sweet, shallow kisses.

"*This* is what I meant when I asked you to stay in London with me," I said in between kisses. "Is this discussing it soon enough for you?"

She burst into laughter, and her eyes twinkled as bright as her diamond. "I'd been preparing myself for a long road ahead. My next goal was to get you to see the convenience of living together. I didn't think...I wasn't sure that marriage would ever be on the table. Are you sure this is what you want? I can go slow. We don't have to commit to—"

I cut her off. "I *want* to marry you, Audrey. I know that with every fiber of my being, and going slow isn't going to make me any more committed than I am right now, because I am utterly and hopelessly devoted to you. Surely you know that by now. So unless *you* don't want to get married..."

"I do! I told you the next guy was going to be The One, and I meant it. Because either the next guy was you or it didn't matter who he was. I only ever wanted you. Since that first week in this apartment, it's only been you."

"Thank fuck, because I was likely going to murder another man if he were to touch you. You're mine." I kissed her again, deeper this time, a primal possessive kiss. The kind that was meant to lead to the removal of clothes.

But before I'd managed to strip more than her coat off her shoulders, she broke away. "And babies?" she asked hopefully. "It's not a deal-breaker. I love you too much. I'm willing to make concessions."

It pulled my heart to hear her suggest she'd give up something she wanted so much just to be with me.

But she didn't need to concede anything on this front. I desperately wanted to see her round and swollen with my child. Wanted to look down at my infant's tiny face and see the perfect blend of features of hers with mine.

Though, I did wince a bit at the prospect of sleepless nights and dirty nappies. "Could we maybe just start with one and see how it goes?"

"We can definitely *start* with one," she said, with a devilish grin. The kind of grin that told me she knew I was wrapped around her little finger and all she had to do was get me to agree to *start* and from there I'd be a goner. "We could start practicing right now even, if you like."

"I'd like that very much."

We lost ourselves in each other then, making love right there on the lounge floor. When we'd finished, we broke open the champagne and fed each other strawberries before I carried her into the bedroom for another round.

Later, as we drifted on the edge of consciousness, it hit me again how close I'd been to losing her. How stupid I'd been and how determined I was to hold onto her now. "How is it possible that you're even here?" I asked, kissing her temple as she lay in my arms. "I tried so hard to set you free."

"And I came back," she replied sleepily. "You know

what that means, right?"

"It's kismet."

Epilogue

Audrey

DYLAN RAN HIS palm along my outer thigh, his gaze pinned on our reflection in the full-length mirror. "You're so fucking sexy. Look at you take my cock like that. Such a good girl."

I let out a breathy moan. Wow, he felt good. Better than ever.

I was bent over the end of the bed, one of the few positions I found comfortable these days, and my husband was pushing into me from behind. We'd recently discovered we could watch ourselves in the mirror from here, and Dylan loved that.

I loved it too, but I was such a horny sex kitten lately that I didn't care where we were doing it, as long as we were doing it. Dylan had yet to complain.

"Stop teasing," I whined, urging him to go faster. "Give it to me already."

Despite my pleas, he dragged his cock out of my body

all the way to the tip.

"Patience, my love. This is too good to rush."

I glanced at him in the reflection. His eyes were dark and focused as he slid back into me, just as slow as before.

"Are you watching this, Audrey? Look how wet you are. You can see it on my dick."

This time when he pulled out, I could see the gleam of dripping moisture on his cock.

"Unf," I gasped. "That *is* hot." I stared magnetically as he repeated his leisure thrust and drag. My belly tightened deep inside as the beginnings of an orgasm formed just from watching the erotic scene.

It was followed by a cramp that wrapped from my lower back around to the front of my torso. That was the downside of pregnant sex—many of my orgasms had been accompanied by uterus contractions since twenty-four weeks.

Which was why Dylan needed to hurry up, titillating as it was to watch the current pace. "But I'm not going to be able to keep this up long, and I need you to bang me good."

"Yes, yes, you're right." He dug his fingers into my hips and notched up the tempo to a steady, moderate pulse.

The tingling knot of arousal began to build and spread at an agonizingly sluggish rate. "Harder," I begged. "Really pound into me."

I wasn't usually so bossy during sex. Dylan knew how to read me without me having to say the words. As I'd neared the end of my pregnancy, though, he'd become more tentative.

"I don't want to hurt you. Are you sure this is okay for the babies?" But he thrust faster anyway, pounding into me so hard, our thighs slapped together.

That was hot too. So hot.

"The babies are fine. Keep this up and Mama will be fine too." More than fine. I sighed with pleasure. A sigh that quickly turned into a whimper as a cramp jolted across my middle. I clutched my hand to the side of my expansive belly.

Dylan noticed and immediately halted. "What's wrong?"

"A cramp. That's all. Keep going."

"Do you want me to—?"

I cut him off. "Don't you *dare* stop!" I pushed my hips back, bouncing on his erection. If he wasn't going to take my need seriously, I was going to do it myself.

"Fuuuuccccckkkk. That's so hot, chasing after my cock like that. Your tits look so fucking fantastic right now. Such a dirty, sweet girl." He was so turned on, he forgot about his concern and drove into me like I wanted. Like I needed. Hammering into me until we exploded simultaneously into orgasm.

Dylan leaned over my backside, and placed light kisses over my shoulders. "I'm going to miss this. We need to get in as much of this as possible before Aaron gets here for Christmas, because after the girls are born, who knows when we'll get to be intimate."

"Oh, please." I shrugged him off so I could roll over and collapse on my back on the bed. "We're still going to have sex after the babies are born. I don't know how many times I have to tell you this. I can't live without it."

He stretched out on the bed next to me on his side and rubbed a hand over my stomach. "I'm not disagreeing that you are a greedy girl when it comes to fucking, but you are vastly underestimating the exhaustion of one baby, let alone twins. I don't know how many times I have to tell you this."

His playful smirk was irresistible, and I couldn't help giggling. "So we'll have to figure out ways to work it in. Sex when we shower. Half-asleep sex. Is it too weird to try to bang while nursing?"

"I am not fucking you while you nurse our daughters. I'm not ever going to be even close to naked around them. That's just...I can't..." His eyes narrowed suddenly. "Ah, I see. You're winding me up."

I lifted up to press a kiss on his lips. "Yes. I'm winding you up. I know it's going to be hard. But I'm young. I'm tough. I'm not worried about it." I stroked the side of his cheek with my fingertips. "Are you worried about it for reals?"

He shook his head. "Not at all."

"And you really don't regret this pregnancy, even though it's two instead of one?"

It was his turn to kiss me. "No regrets. I know better than to argue with what fate has in store for us."

"Good answer." I closed my eyes, relishing the feel of his palm sweeping over my belly. Relishing the awesomeness that was our lives.

Fate really had been good to us. I had never doubted that it would be, but there had definitely been a time when Dylan had. It had been difficult for me to be patient at times. Not all the time, but some of the time. I'd thought about him so much after our Thanksgiving tryst in New York City. Wondered about him. Fantasized about him. He'd made a mark in my life, and I'd figured that was all there would ever be. That we'd be two ships that had crossed in the night, never to meet again.

But then, when I'd found out I'd gotten an internship in the same city he lived in—an internship I hadn't even remembered applying for—I'd been sure that fate had a plan for us. I wasn't sure what the plan was, though, and after countless speeches from Sabrina about how easily I fell in love, I'd tried to steer a course that protected my heart. Dylan had been more than clear that he didn't want a future with anyone, let alone me, and not being willing to lose him from my life all together, I'd believed friendship was the best option for us.

Truth be told, if he'd asked me back to his flat that first night after our reunion, I would have gone in an instant.

But he didn't. His goals hadn't changed, and I'd been determined to accept that. I'd tried *so hard* to accept it.

Except, how could I when he didn't act like that was what he really wanted? He'd jump when I'd call. His gaze would linger. He'd react when we accidentally touched. He'd go out of his way to make sure we accidentally touched.

Maybe it had been wrong to start dating in front of him. I'd been a total tease about it, too, throwing the random guys I encountered in his face, as though they'd meant something to me. As though they could ever possibly mean something to me. I'd wanted him jealous. I'd wanted him as crazed over me as I was becoming over him, whether there was a happy ending for us or not.

When he'd pulled away from our friendship, I'd had to face reality—yes, Dylan was affected by me, but not enough to do anything about it. I figured his attraction must have been physical only. I told myself I should let it go, let him walk away. I told myself to find another guy for real.

I couldn't do it. I'd already become too hung up on him. So I tempted fate. I offered him the one thing that I knew would confuse my heart the most—I offered him a sexual relationship. And while I fell more and more in love with him, all I could do was hope beyond hope that the stars had something in store for us that I couldn't begin to imagine.

The universe delivered tenfold.

We were married in May, in between shows at the Gallery, just five months after he'd proposed. Unbeknownst to us, I was already one month pregnant at the time. We didn't find out until after our honeymoon, a week spent in the beautiful countryside of Southampton where Dylan had been born. We didn't find out we were expecting two girls until late July. To my delight, my husband took the news beautifully. *"I could never imagine being so happy and blessed,"* he'd said.

I couldn't have agreed more.

Still rubbing my stomach, Dylan's lips pressed against my temple. "Do you realize today is the one-year anniversary of our engagement? And here we are getting ready for our girls to arrive in another month. So much has changed in this year, hasn't it?"

I opened my eyes to look at him. At exactly the same moment, my belly tightened with another cramp, and I winced.

His hand stilled. "Damn. I felt that. Is that a contraction?"

"No," I said dismissively. "I mean, yes, but just Braxton Hicks. You know I get these after sex all the time."

Another cramp shot across my middle, winding around my torso. "Oh my fudge," I groaned. This one was painful.

"Are you sure that—"

Before he could finish his thought, a gush of water ran down my legs.

"Your water just broke. Oh, my God, Audrey! Your water just broke!"

Oh, huh. Hadn't been expecting that.

I sat up to look at the mess between my legs. My pulse quickened excitedly and my eyes went wide. "It's time! Oh, my gosh, Dylan! It's time!"

Dylan jumped up and ran to the bathroom, returning a second later with a towel. "This isn't good," he muttered as he cleaned me up. "I knew sex was a bad idea. I shouldn't have gone so hard. We shouldn't have been fucking at all this close to the due date! It's too early. They aren't due for another four weeks!"

"Honey," I said patiently. I said it again when he didn't give me his attention. And a third time. I put my hand on his forearm to get his attention. When he finally looked at me, his eyes blinking rapidly, I continued. "Due in three and a half weeks, actually. We're almost at thirty-seven weeks. The doctor said if we made it to thirty-six weeks with twins it would be fine. We're fine."

"We're fine," he repeated unconvincingly.

"We're going to be fine."

"It's fine." He seemed somewhat calmer. As calm as to be expected, anyway.

"Now, could you maybe move so I can get up and we can both throw some clothes on and head to the hospital?"

"Right, right. Hospital. Right." He started for the dresser, but then immediately turned around and came back to me. He took my face in his hands and kissed me. "I love you. All three of you, but right now I especially love you."

I beamed up at him. "I love you too. So much. Are you scared?" I was. Well, excited *and* scared.

He grinned back at me. "Terrified. Now let's go do this. Let's go meet our daughters. It can't be a coincidence that they've decided to come on this anniversary."

"Of course it's not. It's kismet."

Acknowledgments and Author's Note

It's been a long time since I've enjoyed writing a story as much as I enjoyed writing this one. Audrey is such a breath of fresh air. It's hard not to be happy and humming when in her world. But it's Dylan who stole my heart. His grumpy cat soul is such a kindred spirit, and, writing him, I was able to remember the passion that I had in younger years, able to bring it into my life again in subtle ways. He definitely made a difficult journey out of the dark night into the sun, and I feel like he dragged me right along with him.

On another note for those who might find this interesting, Aaron's cellulitis came directly from personal experience. I was writing Forever with You at the time and was hospitalized for a very scary face infection. It was painful, and I was too miserable at the time to focus on the possible outcomes, though my husband was pretty darn terrified through the whole ordeal. It was particularly harrowing when the first antibiotic I was on wasn't working and the swelling reached the tip of my nose and the outer corners of my eyes. The medical staff greatly feared a brain infection was on the horizon. After it appeared I was on the road to recovery, one doctor said to me, "Thank God for antibiotics. This would have killed you a hundred years ago." Yes. Thank God for antibiotics.

As always, my heart is full of gratitude for a gaggle of people.

My sweet, kickass team, Candi Kane, Melissa Gaston—nothing is possible without you two. You're as much Laurelin Paige as I am. Thank you for always being by my side, encouraging me, ranting with me, sharing all your love. Thank you for being two of my best friends.

Kayti McGee, my other half and plot submissive—you're the Audrey to my Dylan. You fucking ray of sunshine. (Ferda).

Rebecca Friedman my sweet friend (and agent!). I'm more grateful for your presence in my life than you could ever know.

Amy "Vox" Libris and Roxie Madar—you ladies push me in the most delicious ways. Thank you for putting up with my plot talks and my constant need for validation.

Erica Russikoff—this past May, my life coach (yes, I'm one of those people) told me I needed to find an editor who loved my words and felt as passionate about the stories I wanted to tell as I did. I hadn't even set out on the search yet when Erica approached me at a signing, and she is EVERYTHING I could want in a collaborator and more. From now on, Erica. Always, always Erica.

Michele Ficht—thank you for finding all my flaws. You're absolutely flawless.

Andi Arndt and Marni Coleman at Lyric Audio and Carly Robins and Shane East—what a fantastic group to be working with! Thank you for all the eargasms.

Alyssa Garcia at Uplifting Designs for giving character to the pages.

Lauren Blakely—you're my friend, but also my mentor. You can't know how giddy I get when I wake up to voice messages from you, left while you're walking your dogs. You have so many inspiring thoughts, and it's a privilege to get to be part of your brainstorming. Thanks so much for all the guidance on the audio for these, and for so many other things that it's an incredible job to even try to catalog.

Sadia Ashraf and Gina Goff—I'm so thrilled to be on this new adventure with you ladies. I can't wait for what's on the horizon.

My LARCS and my Instagram team—you ladies make magic happen, and I'll never stop being grateful.

The Sky Launchers—your enthusiasm for my work is humbling and healing. Thank you.

My readers all around the world—thank you for this wild ride you've let me take. You make my life incredible.

My Snatches, Melanie Harlow, Kayti McGee, Sierra Simone—true sisters for life. #snakes #neverforget

Emma Hart—it's like old times, except you're telling me the British words for things instead of vice versa. Thanks for being my source across the pond.

Liz and Steve Berry—such good hosts, such great friends, such good people. Nineteen years looks good on you. Jillian Stein, you're automatically included when I mention Liz. Do you even exist separately?

CD Reiss—whatever happens next in your career, you must always continue to let me burden you with the tough discussions of our time. There's no one who looks as thoroughly at the "issues" as you do, and I'm so grateful to be able to bounce my worst thoughts in your direction.

My mother, husband, and daughters—what a crazy, kooky bunch you are! I love you all and can't imagine our lives any other way.

My God—you never fail to turn my darkness into light. (Psalms 18:28)

There are more dirty men in my universe.

And they all have filthy, rich love stories to share.

Dirty Duet - Donovan Kincaid

Dirty Filthy Rich Men

Dirty Filthy Rich Love

Available Now!

Dirty Games Duet - Weston King

Dirty Sexy Player

Dirty Sexy Games

Available Now!

Dirty Filthy Fix - Nate Sinclair

Available Now!

Dirty Wild Duet - Cade Warren

Coming in 2020

Also by Laurelin Paige

Visit my website, laurelinpaige.com, for a more detailed reading order.

The Fixed Universe

Fixed Series
Fixed on You
Found in You
Forever with You
Hudson
Fixed Forever

Found Duet

Free Me
Find Me
Chandler (a spinoff novel)
Falling Under You (a spinoff novella)
Dirty Filthy Fix (a spinoff novella)

Slay Trilogy

Slay One
Slay Two (fall 2019)
Slay Three (winter 2019)
Slay Four (spring 2020)

First and Last

First Touch
Last Kiss

Spark - short, steamy sparks of romance

One More Time

Ryder Brothers

Close
Want by Kayti McGee
More by JD Hawkins

Hollywood Heat

Sex Symbol
Star Struck

Written with Sierra Simone

Porn Star
Hot Cop

Written with Kayti McGee under the name Laurelin McGee

Miss Match
Love Struck
MisTaken
Holiday for Hire

About Laurelin Paige

With over 2.4 million books sold worldwide, Laurelin Paige is a New York Times, Wall Street Journal and USA Today Bestselling Author. Her international success started with her very first series, the Fixed Trilogy, which, alone, has sold over 1 million copies, and earned her the coveted #1 spot on Amazon's bestseller list in the U.S., U.K., Canada, and Australia, simultaneously. This title also was named in People magazine as one of the top 10 most downloaded books of 2014. She's also been #1 over all books at the Apple Book Store with more than one title in more than one country. She's published both independently and with MacMillan's St. Martin's Press and Griffin imprints as well as many other publishers around the world including Harper Collins in Germany and Hachette/Little Brown in the U.K. With her edgy, trope-flipped stories of smart women and strong men, she's managed to secure herself among today's romance royalty.

Paige has a Bachelor's degree in Musical Theater and a Masters of Business Administration with a Marketing emphasis, and she credits her writing success to what she learned from both programs, though she's also an avid learner, constantly trying to challenge her mind with new and exciting ideas and concepts. While she loves psychological thrillers and witty philosophical books and entertainment, she is a sucker for a good romance and gets giddy anytime there's kissing, much to the embarrassment of her three daughters. Her husband doesn't seem to complain, however. When she isn't reading or writing sexy stories, she's probably singing, watching Game of Thrones or The Walking Dead, or dreaming of Michael Fassbender.

She's also a proud member of Mensa International though she doesn't do anything with the organization except use it as material for her bio. She currently lives outside Austin, Texas and is represented by Rebecca Friedman.

Visit www.laurelinpaige.com to find out more about my books and sign up for my newsletter.

Want to be notified when I have a new release?

Text Paige to 21000, and I'll shoot you a text when I have a book come out.

Made in the USA
Middletown, DE
06 July 2020